PARADISE

BY
SHIRLEY KEMP

MILLS & BOON LIMITED
ETON HOUSE   18-24 PARADISE ROAD
RICHMOND   SURREY   TW9 1SR

*First published in Great Britain 1992
by Mills & Boon Limited*

© Shirley Kemp 1992

*Australian copyright 1992
Philippine copyright 1992
This edition 1992*

ISBN 0 263 77764 2

*Set in Times Roman 10½ on 12 pt.
01-9210-50377 C*

Made and printed in Great Britain

CHAPTER ONE

JENNA swerved to avoid the huge boulder which loomed with frightening suddenness around the final twist in the sharp double bend of the road, but the near side of the car struck the jagged stone a wrenching blow.

The sound of the crash reverberated around the valley.

Suzie, startled awake by the jolt, was staring up at her sister with large, frightened blue eyes.

'Oh, Jenna! What's happened.'

'Just a stone in the road, darling,' Jenna soothed. 'Nothing to worry about. Are you hurt?'

'I don't know. My head hurts.'

'Where?' Keep calm, Jenna, she told herself as she saw the lump on Suzie's temple. It seemed to be growing before her anxious eyes. 'Does it hurt much?' She put her fingers gingerly to the discoloured skin.

Suzie flinched. 'It does a bit. And my head feels funny.'

'Funny?' Jenna echoed, trying to keep her voice level. 'Do you feel sleepy?'

'A bit.' As though her words were a cue, Suzie's large blue eyes began to close.

'Don't go to sleep.' Jenna tried to keep the note of panic from her voice as she tried to remember what little she knew of first aid. If it was concussion, weren't you supposed to keep the person awake? 'Are you hurt anywhere else?'

'I don't know.' Suzie was sinking back into her seat and Jenna reached over to examine her and winced as a shaft of pain shot through her left wrist. Her hand felt numb and useless and she groaned. All she needed at this point in time was a broken wrist, she thought irritably. But, for now, it was her little sister who was of prime concern.

'Does it hurt anywhere else?'

Jenna ran her good hand over the small thin body and sighed with relief as the little girl murmured sleepily, 'No. Only my head.'

'Try to stay awake, Suzie, while I try and think what to do next.'

Jenna moved experimentally. Apart from the painful wrist, she seemed to be all in one piece.

She tried to open the car door but it jammed halfway.

Jenna grimaced in exasperation and slumped back into her seat. They really were in a bit of a mess. The roads they'd traversed for the past hour had been a nightmare. Narrow, rough and stony, with deep potholes gouged from the surface, no doubt by the torrents of rain which must rush down from the steep rocky ridges towering above. It had probably been the last heavy rainfall which had dislodged the fateful boulder and sent it rolling into the road.

With a sick sensation, she realised that if she'd swerved much further to the right they would have gone careering down into the valley below.

Jenna shivered. The place seemed bleak, particularly now, when the air was filled with a faint misty rain. The ridge above cut out what light there was and the road had a slight but terrifying camber, which seemed to draw the small car towards the abyss of the

steep valley which fell away to the right. The
countryside rolled away for miles, empty and desolate, and Jenna guessed that the chances of another
motorist coming along this isolated route must be
pretty slim.

She sighed heavily. In a few minutes, when she had
recovered her wits, she would have to try again to get
out and take a look at the damage. Perhaps she would
be able to catch a glimpse of a house somewhere in
the sweep of the valley.

'Are you all right?'

The suddenness with which the ghostly figure appeared at the half-open door of the car startled her
into a gasp.

'My God! Where did you spring from?'

'I heard the crunch of metal from lower down the
valley.' The man was panting, as though he'd run for
some distance. 'Is anyone hurt?'

'My sister, Suzie, has a nasty bump on the head,
which hopefully isn't too serious.' Jenna felt weak with
relief at their unexpected rescue. 'And my wrist feels
a bit numb. Other than that, we seem to be OK.'

'Thank heaven for that.'

Jenna heard his deep sigh and peered at him curiously. His face was partly hidden by the upturned
collar of his jacket, pulled up high to keep out the
misty rain, but in this light he looked pale and shaken.
His dark eyes looked strained as he surveyed her
through the window.

'Let's take a look at the child first, then I'll see to
your hand.'

He went around to the passenger door, which
seemed undamaged.

Suzie's large blue eyes opened and she stared at him as he leant over her, his large hands gently exploring the lump on her head and her thin wiry frame.

'She seems all right,' he pronounced with a grunt of satisfaction. 'But that bump on the head needs to be looked at by a doctor.'

'Do you think she's got concussion?' Jenna asked anxiously. 'She seems very sleepy.'

'It's a possibility. She hasn't wanted to be sick, has she?'

'No.' Jenna answered faintly.

'Good. Well, let's hope for the best.' He came back around the car to Jenna.

'Let me take a quick look at the wrist.'

The stranger held out his hand and Jenna put her own meekly into it. He examined it deftly, his large hands unexpectedly gentle and comforting.

After a minute or two, he lowered her hand into her lap. 'I don't think it's broken, but I'm no expert, and the doctor will need to take a look at that too.'

His eyes held hers briefly as he studied her face and Jenna was struck once again by the strain apparent on his strong features. For some reason, she couldn't hold his narrowed gaze and dropped her head, feeling an unaccustomed warmth creeping into her cheeks.

With the door open, Jenna could see their rescuer was a big man. Even though he was crouching, his bulk filled the narrow aperture. It was getting dusk and from the glistening droplets of water trapped in the dark hair, which peeped from beneath his hat, it seemed the rain was beginning to fall in earnest.

'That scarf you're wearing will make a fine sling for your wrist until the doctor can take a look at it.'

'I'm very relieved to see you,' Jenna ventured gratefully as he leaned towards her. 'And surprised. This seems like the middle of nowhere.'

'It is!' He laughed, a short harsh sound. 'You're lucky I was within hearing distance, or you might have had to stay here until morning. Glenrae is miles away and no one uses this road at night.'

His fingers were cold against her throat as he undid the small brooch she'd used to fasten the scarf at her neckline. She shivered. This close, he emitted a powerful vibration which shortened her breath, but he seemed unaware of her reaction as he tied and adjusted the scarf to hold her wrist.

'That should do it.' He stood up, pushing his hands into the small of his back to ease the tension of crouching.

'Thank you. I'm very grateful.'

'No thanks needed.' An impatient wave of his hand brushed her words aside.

His smile seemed more of an irritated grimace, Jenna thought, as she peered curiously at his strong, lean profile. He looked grim and anxious and his face was unnaturally pale.

'I'll have to leave you for a while,' he said. 'But I'll be back. Sit tight and relax.'

He vanished quickly, leaving Jenna to wonder who he was and how he'd come to be so miraculously on the spot.

She turned her attention to Suzie. The little girl was asleep, nestled down into the seat, and Jenna wondered anxiously whether she should wake her. The bump seemed to have swollen to its full potential and was now badly discoloured. But her cheeks had recovered their colour and her breathing was peaceful.

Jenna gathered her sister comfortably against her and settled back to wait for the return of the stranger.

The sky was becoming progressively darker and a thin, chill wind blew in through the gaping door. She was trembling, probably with delayed shock as well as the cold, and, with her good hand she gathered her jacket more closely about her.

Mercifully, it wasn't too long before she saw fingers of light pointing upwards, etched against the darkened sky, and her heart lifted as a vehicle came slowly towards them. Beyond the glare of its headlights, she identified the silhouette of their rescuer as he alighted from what looked, in the gloom, to be a Land Rover.

He strode across to her and tugged the car door wider.

'Sorry you had to wait,' he said, as Jenna, after moving Suzie gently away, began to slide out of her seat. 'I was further away than I remembered. When I heard the crash my first thought was to get here and I dashed up the ridge on foot instead of driving around.'

'I'm glad you did.' Jenna winced as the movement of getting out jarred her wrist.

'Take it easy.' His large hand came around her waist, the other cupping her elbow to hold her arm steady.

Jenna felt the disturbing electricity of the man and bit her lip, trying to give her full attention to the problem of getting out of the car. Once she was out, her legs betrayed her as she tried to stand. His hand tightened about her, holding her firmly to his lean frame.

'Can you walk? You seem as weak as a baby.' His voice was gentle with concern and had a strange effect on Jenna's insides.

'It's probably the shock,' she muttered in embarrassment. 'I'm not usually this much of a wimp.'

He laughed shortly. 'I'm sure of that.'

From his tone, Jenna wasn't quite sure how to take that, but she didn't have time to dwell on it. Even his laugh had her tingling, and she was filled with astonishment at her uncharacteristic responsiveness to this unknown stranger.

With her feelings so volatile, it would be better to keep her distance. 'I . . . I think I can manage alone.'

He took his hands away and she swayed.

'Ach!' He exclaimed, in sudden impatience. 'Let's have ye up here.' The merest trace of a Scottish accent sounded in his voice, enhancing its deep masculinity.

As though she were feather-light, he swung her easily into his arms, and Jenna had to fight an almost overwhelming urge to nestle her head into the hollow between his throat and broad shoulder. The tweed fabric of his jacket was rough against her cheek and had a peculiarly masculine scent that was somehow comforting.

It was amazing, but she felt like a child, vulnerable and in need of reassurance, but the tight expression on his face, hard and somehow remote, reminded her of the glowering rocky ridge behind them.

'You can put me down now,' she said, her voice sounding angry. 'I'm sure I'll be all right, thank you.'

He ignored her remark, carrying her easily across to his vehicle and lowering her, without effort, into the front seat. He left her and came back seconds later with Suzie in his arms, still fast asleep. He put

her down gently on the back seat, where she immediately curled up.

Jenna cast an anxious glance at her sister, mut-
tering a silent prayer. Please God, let her be all right.
There'd been enough disaster in the past year or so
for both of them.

She shrugged the gloomy thoughts away, trying to
see the positive side. At least they were both still in
one piece. And they'd had a bit of luck in the shape
of the stranger.

Their rescuer got into the driving seat beside Jenna.
'Your car will be safe enough there for tonight,' he
said, as he began to back his vehicle along the narrow
road. 'I'll organise someone to move it in the morning
and get that boulder out of the way.'

He sounded clipped and competent and Jenna
thought sourly that he was obviously the kind of man
who was used to taking charge.

'Thank you,' she muttered in a subdued voice,
feeling foolish about her earlier outburst.

The road widened, enabling him to turn his vehicle
around, and Jenna held her breath as they seemed,
for a moment, to teeter on the brink of the abyss. But
his large hands competently spun the wheel and soon
they were heading away from the scene of her disaster.

Jenna wanted to feel grateful, but was a little intimidated by the grimness of his face, as he concentrated on the road ahead. It wasn't the face of a man
who enjoyed small talk, she decided, so it seemed best
just to sit quietly beside him, swaying to the gentle,
almost mesmeric movements of the big Land Rover,
trying hard to ignore her sharp awareness of him.

Despite the spacious front seating, he seemed to fill
all the available room, his shoulder unavoidably close

to hers. Even through the thick, damp material of his jacket, she felt the tingling vibrations of his powerful personality. She was tempted to lean on him, to place her aching head against his arm.

The temptation shocked her. She wasn't the type to lean on the nearest available male when things went wrong, and she could only put her present trembling weakness down to the effects of shock, but the sensation of his arms holding her still persisted.

'What were you doing on these roads at this time of the evening?'

The enquiry was mild enough, but Jenna was shaken by the look of strong disapproval on his face.

'I'm making for Glenrae,' she said, sounding defensive. 'My aunt and cousin have a riding school there. My sister and I are going to help out for the summer.'

There was no mistaking the sudden stiffening of his back, nor the grim set of his jaw. 'Your aunt being Louise Anderson?'

The question seemed to hang in the air like an accusation, making Jenna answer with uncharacteristic diffidence. 'Yes. Do you know her?'

He gave a harsh laugh, which, for some reason, made the nerves at the back of her neck tingle. 'Oh, yes. That I do.'

Jenna frowned. The words, in themselves, meant nothing, but the tone was distinctly unfriendly.

'Are you . . . a neighbour?'

He turned on her a brief, searching stare, which disconcerted her even more than his words.

'I'm Duncan Fergusson. And I suppose you could say I'm a neighbour of your aunt's, though only as the crow flies.'

His eyes were back on the road, but the memory of their burning intensity remained to puzzle Jenna.

'Do you live in Glenrae?' she probed the puzzle.

'Yes. But a few miles outside the village, I'm glad to say.' He shot her a quick glance. 'You've never been here before?'

'No. I haven't seen my aunt for many years. Not since she remarried and came to live in Glenrae, when I was a child.'

'It can't have been that many years.' His laugh sounded almost amused. 'You're not much more than a child now.'

Jenna bristled. 'I'm nearly twenty-four. Hardly a child.'

He laughed again. 'Of course. You're right. Twenty-four is ancient, but you don't look it.'

'Thank you.' Jenna said, a little sceptically. If she didn't look her age, then it was a miracle, given the heartache of the recent past.

Encouraged a little by his laugh, Jenna asked. 'What's Glenrae like?'

He considered her question for a moment or two before answering.

'Well, like every village, I suppose, a small place, where everyone knows everyone.' He made a derisory sound. 'And everyone else's business too, as you'll no doubt find out shortly.'

He turned again, briefly, his eyes flicking over her troubled face. 'What's your name?'

'Jenna Wilde,' she replied and then indicated her sleeping sister. 'This is my sister Suzie.'

'Hmph! The name suits you.' He said wryly. 'It would take someone half wild to be driving on these treacherous roads so close to dusk. It would have been more sensible to stick to the main roads.'

'I did,' she replied hotly. 'But somewhere along the line I must have taken a wrong turning.'

'Several, I should think.' He laughed grimly. 'Didn't that cousin of yours, Stuart Anderson, give you any idea of the safe route?'

'I'm quite capable of working out my own route, thank you.'

'Oh, aye! I had you down for headstrong the first minute I set eyes on you.' He shot her a hard, disparaging look. 'But, in this instance, you would have done better to seek advice. This part of the country is harsh and, as you've learned the hard way, it can be very dangerous.'

The description could be aptly applied to the inhabitants of the place as well, Jenna thought mutinously.

'It wasn't my fault there was a boulder around a bend in the road. The accident could have happened to anyone.'

'Anyone with an ounce of common sense wouldn't have been anywhere near that road close to dark. But then, common sense is hardly a strong point in your family.'

Jenna coloured hotly and clenched her fists, fighting an uncharacteristic impulse to strike him. She took a deep breath and counted slowly to ten. Then she said, as evenly as she could through the hard knot of anger that had formed in her throat, 'I've been driving since early morning. Glenrae is less than an hour away and if I hadn't had the bad luck to hit that boulder I should have been there well before dark.'

Her voice trembled on the last words, as she realised how close she had come to arriving safely at her destination. It was just damned hard luck she'd hit the boulder . . . the same hard luck that had been dogging her footsteps for so long. The same hard luck that had been responsible for her losing her teaching job and which now had turned her handsome Good Samaritan into a bitter accuser, with some kind of chip on his shoulder.

'I'm grateful for your help, but that doesn't give you the right to criticise me or members of my family.'

She glared at him and he turned to catch her gaze. The grim look seemed to have disappeared, to be replaced by an appraisal which was just as disconcerting.

'Well. You seem to have more guts than most of them.'

He turned away and relapsed into silence, leaving Jenna feeling confused and uncertain.

Fortunately, he seemed now to need all of his powers of concentration to negotiate the road which had become, once again, narrow and rocky.

After travelling for some time in silence, Jenna found the nerve to speak again. 'Are we close to my aunt's house?'

'No. But we're very close to my place and that's where you'll stop the night. I'll have Dr McRae call in to take a look at the young lass and he can check on your hand at the same time.'

'Oh, but I don't want to put you to any trouble,' Jenna said in dismay.

'It's no trouble.'

They had come to a junction in the road and he slowed to take the left-hand fork. They seemed to be heading upwards again, curving back towards the towering ridge, and Jenna was gripped suddenly with an alarming feeling that she was being transported across some unseen point of no return.

'I'd prefer to go to my aunt's at Glenrae,' she said, trying to hide the note of panic in her voice, adding through her teeth, 'If you don't mind.'

'But I do mind.' In the dim light, Jenna witnessed again the hardening of his craggy handsome face. 'We go where I say, unless you want to get out and walk.'

For one insane second, Jenna thought wildly of doing just that, but realised immediately that, much as she hated his brute forcefulness, she had no alternative but to stay where she was. She and Suzie were completely in his hands and there was nothing she could do about it.

The dim grey light revealed the aggressive thrust of his slightly curved nose, balanced by the rock-like chin. His wide generous mouth, which had seemed sensitive and gentle as he'd attended to her wrist, was clamped now into a hard line as he looked rigidly ahead. She sensed, with a shiver, that he would make a ruthless and determined adversary.

He said no more, obviously thinking he had said all that was necessary. Jenna wished it were possible to put up some kind of a fight, if only to salvage some remnant of her pride, but she knew it was useless. All she could hope for was that, at some time in the future, she might find a way of proving to him that she wasn't the kind to be so easily beaten.

She bit her lip to stop herself giving voice to the vengeful thought, and sank deeper into her seat.

Jenna must have dozed. She woke, startled, as the vehicle drew to a halt, and it was mortifying to dis-

cover that her head was against his shoulder. She
moved quickly away.

He switched off the engine and doused the lights
and, as Jenna's eyes grew accustomed to the gloom,
she peered curiously out as a large building became
discernible. From her rescuer's appearance, she had
been expecting a cottage, possibly a farmhouse. She
was totally unprepared for the imposing grandeur of
the house which met her gaze as he lifted her out on
to her feet.

'Do you need to be carried again?' he enquired with
a hint of irony.

'No, thank you,' she answered positively. 'I can
manage alone.'

'Good.' His dismissal was almost insulting, and
Jenna smouldered with resentment.

He turned his attention to Suzie, still sleeping in
the back of the car. As he touched her, the little girl
stirred and began to stretch, opening dazed and sleepy
eyes. Jenna watched as for a moment he hesitated, as
though reluctant to lift the small, huddled figure, but
in the next instant he'd swept her up into his arms,
leaving Jenna to wonder if she'd imagined that momentary hesitation.

He carried Suzie towards the house. Jenna, following unsteadily in his wake, was filled with a sudden
apprehension. A family visit, which had promised to
be a pleasant interlude, seemed suddenly fraught with
danger.

He led the way into a large, warm kitchen, where
a round-faced woman presided over an enormous
black range.

'Ah! Master Duncan! We were wondering when
ye'd turn up for supper,' she began and stopped as

she saw Suzie in his arms. 'Good lord above! What have ye there?'

'A couple of lassies who've had an accident out on the ridge, Annie,' he answered shortly, handing Suzie into her plump arms. 'I'm off to ring Dr McRae. Get Mary to see to putting the little one to bed and then find a bowl of broth or something for the other.'

Listening to his peremptory commands, Jenna felt her hackles rise. He was ordering their disposal as if they were two unwanted waifs he'd picked up along his way.

'An accident, ye say?' The older woman called Annie hugged Suzie close, a look of consternation robbing her rosy cheeks of their glow. 'Is the bairn hurt badly?'

'Don't fret, Annie.' He put a surprisingly gentle hand on her shoulder. 'There's no real harm done, as far as I can gather. But I'll get McRae over here just to be sure.'

'Aye. That's best.'

Duncan Fergusson left the room without even a glance at Jenna, who stood smouldering with resentment and gazing about uncertainly.

'Sit ye down, dearie,' Annie said. 'I'll pass the wee lass to Mary and then I'll be back to look after you.'

As she left the room with Suzie in her arms, Jenna sank down into a small over-stuffed armchair by the warm range, aware of an almost overwhelming weakness. Annie's promise to look after her had brought unusual tears to her eyes. It seemed so long since anyone had cared.

She leaned back in the comfortable chair and closed her eyes, letting her fatigue take over, and must have dozed. From far away, she heard the voice of her rescuer, but found it impossible to lift her weighted lids.

'Looks like you're too late with the broth, Annie. She's asleep.'

'Ah! Exhausted, poor lass, and her hardly more than a child.'

'Aye. But don't let that angel face fool you. I've had a glimpse behind, to the heart of a tiger.'

'And that's no more than a woman would need to be dealing with a man like you, Master Duncan.'

He laughed, a strangely pleasant sound that, even in her semi-conscious state, had Jenna's insides fluttering.

She felt herself lifted and carried, her oddly weighted head against the hollow of his shoulder. And then she was lying somewhere soft and comfortable as someone gently took the clothes from her and slipped something cool over her head and eased it beneath her oddly helpless body.

She felt herself sinking ever deeper into a delicious lethargy. Did she really feel the cool, light touch of a lean hand against her forehead . . . the gentle swift caress of fingers brushing damp tendrils from her cheeks? Or was it the beginning of a wonderful soothing dream?

CHAPTER TWO

JENNA woke to unfamiliar sounds and strong sunlight streaming through a wide window. The curtains had been pulled back and she could glimpse the leafy branches of a tall tree brushing against the pane.

For a few minutes, she had trouble remembering where she was before recalling, with a groan, that she'd crashed the car and had been forced to accept the hospitality of a dour and critical stranger.

Her head was stiff and faintly muzzy, as though she were suffering from some kind of over-indulgence, and her wrist throbbed dully as she tried to lift it. She felt helpless and useless and rather bad-tempered and she wondered anxiously how Suzie was. She really ought to get up and find out, but her strength seemed to be slow in returning.

She had just decided she would make the effort to get up anyway, when the door opened suddenly to admit a white-haired man with ruddy cheeks and a bristling, yellow-tinged moustache. He advanced purposefully into the room, nodding his large head and smiling encouragingly at Jenna, who fixed wondering eyes on his genial face.

'Hello, m'dearie,' he said. 'How are you doing this morning? I called in last night, but ye were fast asleep. I had a quick look at ye then, but thought it best to leave a proper examination until this morning.'

'You're Dr McRae?'

He nodded. 'Aye. The very same.'

Jenna sighed with relief. 'Oh, good! Have you seen my sister Suzie?'

'I have indeed.'

'How is she? That awful bump——' she began anxiously.

'Looks worse than it is,' he cut in reassuringly. 'Give the lassie a couple of days to rest and I'm sure she'll be fine.' He bent over her. 'Now let's have a look at you.'

His hands were large and competent as he examined her thoroughly and Jenna was relieved to see his smiling nod of satisfaction as he completed his task and stood up.

'Well, no bones broken. That wrist will be a bit painful for a while, but there's nothing amiss that won't mend quickly.'

Jenna smiled. 'Then I'll be able to go on to my aunt's today?'

'Ye've had a nasty experience.' He frowned. 'Ye might be better to stay put for a day or so. Let the shock work its way out, as much for yourself as the little girl.' He patted her shoulder in a comforting gesture.

'But my aunt will be worried——'

He held up his hand to halt her protest.

'I'm sure your aunt will be happy enough when she knows you're both in such good hands.'

'My aunt is Louise Anderson. She was expecting me and Suzie yesterday,' she protested. 'She's probably already anxious not to have heard from us.'

'Louise Anderson, ye say.' The doctor looked at her in a way that seemed distinctly odd. 'Ye're Louise Anderson's niece.'

Jenna nodded. 'Yes. Suzie and I are here to help out at the riding school for the summer.'

'I see.' He nodded his large head, his hand massaging the crease that had appeared between his brows with a disbelieving expression that puzzled Jenna. He roused himself, rubbing his hands together as though disposing of a problem. 'Ah, well! I'm sure Duncan would already have contacted Louise to tell her of your accident.'

Jenna gave a grim little laugh. 'Well, at least you don't seem to find anything wrong with the name Anderson.'

'Aye. The man finds it hard to forgive.' The old doctor shook his head. 'Understandable in the circumstances, I suppose.'

'What circumstances?' Jenna was quick to interpose. Perhaps now she would hear the reason for Duncan Fergusson's hatred.

'If you don't know, then I'm not the one to tell you.' He patted Jenna's hand. 'Ye'll find out soon enough, I dare say.'

'Perhaps. But not from Duncan Fergusson.' She made an impatient sound. 'Why does he have to be so hard...so difficult?'

'Hard! Yes.' The doctor agreed. 'But only on the surface. Yet ye'll find there's a heart of gold beneath.'

'Only someone would have to be a fool to dig for it.' Jenna retorted with a hint of bitterness, adding almost to herself. 'And whatever else, I hope I'm no fool.'

'I hope not, lassie. Well, not as far as your health is concerned at any rate.' Dr McRae gave her a stern look. 'I'm advising ye rest. See that ye take it.'

He left, and minutes later, after a brief knock, the door opened again and Duncan Fergusson came striding into the room. He looked younger in the clear light of morning. Nearer thirty-two or three than the thirty-eight she'd guessed the night before. And he was even more compelling, she noted with a strange quiver of awareness; he looked muscular and very fit in fawn breeches and highly polished riding boots, and the polo-necked sweater and light tweed jacket set off his wide powerful shoulders.

Jenna remembered that her head had rested against them last night and she felt the colour creeping into her cheeks as he surveyed her silently. His attention made her acutely conscious of the picture she must present, with her golden-brown hair tumbling on the pillow, curling tendrils clinging to her cheeks and into the hollow curve of her shoulder.

His eyes lingered on her throat and she put up her hand defensively, aghast to find that the rather large nightgown Annie must have found for her gaped open, revealing the gentle swell of her breasts. She tugged self-consciously at her neckline, struggling to do up the buttons. But her left hand was still numb and painful and small beads of perspiration broke on her forehead with the effort.

He made a small irritable sound. 'Here, let me.'

Jenna drew a sharp breath. 'I'd rather you didn't.'

'Don't be ridiculous. You're hardly a shy schoolgirl.'

'It's not a question of being shy,' Jenna retorted, stung by the gibe. 'I just happen to be particular.'

'Glad to hear it.'

He brushed her hands away and she was helpless to stop him taking over the task of fastening her buttons. She felt the cool touch of his fingers against her skin, sending strange sensations through her, and she recalled the dream caress of the night before, the memory mingling with her embarrassment to produce a strange disturbance.

But, from his impersonal, faintly irritated expression, he might have been performing the same intimate service for Suzie, or any member of his own household, with the same obvious detachment. His coolness annoyed her, especially since her own reactions to him were presently in danger of overwhelming her.

His head was close to hers and she had a close-up view of the thick dark lashes which fanned across his cheeks, hiding the peculiar dark glow of his eyes. Her heart was pounding uncomfortably and she squirmed, wondering if he could hear its excited hammering. Mercifully, he had finished his self-imposed task and was straightening away from her.

'There! That didn't hurt too much, did it?'

'Thank you.' Her voice was a hoarse croak.

'My pleasure.' The frowning look was back.

'I hardly think my presence is much pleasure to you,' she bit back angrily. 'But I'll relieve you of it as soon as possible.'

His mouth twisted. 'You're planning to leave?'

'Well, of course.' Jenna flushed. 'I'd have liked to go right away, but the doctor seemed to think Suzie should rest for today.'

He grimaced. 'I got the impression her recovery would take a little longer than one day. She's had a nasty bump.'

'Yes, I know.' Jenna nodded. 'But, knowing Suzie, she'll be as bright as a button in the morning.' As she said it, she crossed her fingers and hoped she was right.

'Maybe . . . and maybe not. We shall see.' His gaze flicked across her face. 'Did you sleep well?'

'Well enough.'

Almost absently, he brushed a tendril of hair from her cheek.

The warmth in Jenna's face increased at his touch and she wondered at her own physical responsiveness to him, since she had put men quite positively out of her life. And, besides, his dark rugged looks were definitely not her type.

She had always liked fair-skinned men, with pale silky hair, like Martin . . . She brought herself up with a start. It was ages since she'd allowed the thought of Martin past the sentinel in her brain. Her will-power must be weakening, due, probably, to last night's trauma.

Her attention returned to Duncan Fergusson, who was watching her with cool eyes. Why did he always have to look so damned sure of himself? she wondered resentfully.

But she'd been glad enough to see him last night, when he'd arrived at the scene of their accident, and she ought to be feeling grateful rather than hostile.

'Which reminds me, I haven't thanked you properly for last night,' she said. 'I don't know what would have happened if you hadn't been in the vicinity to come to our rescue.'

'Neither do I,' he agreed blandly. 'And I won't lecture you again about the stupidity of the route you chose.'

'Thank goodness for that,' Jenna said spiritedly. 'Once was more than enough.'

'Then, let's hope you've learned your lesson.' Despite the admonishing words, he surprised her with a smile, which lightened the rugged contours of his face and made him look almost handsome.

Jenna felt the leap of her pulses with self-disgust.

She had a sneaking suspicion that if he put himself out to be charming he would encounter little difficulty in attracting the opposite sex. But last night he had been positively churlish, and the silent voice of reason warned her to be very wary where this man was concerned.

She wondered what he had against her aunt and her cousin. There was obviously some bad blood between him and her family. It could be something and nothing, she reasoned, perhaps the result of a recent disagreement, which would quickly blow over.

Alternatively, it could be an ancient feud between two clans, the echoes of which remained to haunt the present-day descendants. A romantic and unlikely situation, she reasoned, but perhaps still possible.

'Would you mind if I phoned my aunt later?' She didn't want to stir up any problems, but surely his animosity wouldn't deny her the courtesy of a telephone call?

'I spoke to your aunt this morning.' His brow darkened ominously. 'And I let her know, in no uncertain terms, that she's lucky you and your sister have turned up at all.'

Jenna groaned. She had called a truce, but he obviously hadn't. 'That's unfair,' she protested. 'She can hardly be blamed for a boulder in the road.' She propped herself up on one elbow and went on indignantly, 'Except, of course, by an absolute bigot, with an oversized chip on his shoulder.'

Anger flared brightly in his eyes as they scorched into her challenging stare.

'So. I have a chip on my shoulder? Is that what they told you?' He gripped her upper arms.

'They—if you mean my aunt and cousin—told me nothing.' She refused to be intimidated by the steely voice. 'I haven't a clue what this is all about and quite frankly I don't care.'

She began to struggle, but he held her firmly, giving her a little shake.

'And that, if I may say so, is typical of the breed. Selfish, uncaring...'

His grip on her arms increased, until Jenna couldn't hold back her yell of pain.

'Damn you!' she gasped. 'Let me go.'

His face, which had been a mask of anger, suddenly changed, and he relaxed his hold on her.

'I'm sorry,' he said, in a hard clipped voice. 'That shouldn't have happened.'

He got up suddenly and paced to the window, staring out broodingly.

'I think it might be better if Suzie and I did leave this morning,' she said coldly. 'After all, Glenrae isn't at the other end of the world, and if you're too busy to take us I could ask my cousin Stuart to come and collect us.' She saw his spine stiffen. 'I'm sure he wouldn't mind.'

He swung around and Jenna was unprepared for the fury of his expression.

'Stuart Anderson knows better than to turn up here.'

Jenna stared at him for long seconds, wondering what on earth Stuart had done to him to arouse such obvious dislike. Duncan Fergusson was obviously a man of intense feeling who found it difficult to forgive, but surely nothing could be bad enough to warrant this reaction.

'In that case,' she ventured, at last, 'he doesn't have to come to the house. He can pick us up on the road outside. We can wait there for him at whatever time he can manage to come.'

'There's no need for any of that,' he replied in a voice of quiet reason and Jenna was surprised to see no trace of his former anger. His expression was carefully composed as he went on. 'I'll take you myself, but not today. I'm busy and the doctor ordered rest for you.'

'But that's ridiculous!' she protested. 'I can rest at my aunt's house, if I need to. But I'm fine.'

'Are you?' He came and sat on the side of her bed, his narrowed gaze on her face. 'Have you looked in the mirror this morning? You're like a ghost.'

Staring into his face, Jenna saw a flash of emotion that looked like pain, but it was gone so swiftly that she knew she must be mistaken.

He traced long, lean fingers down her cheek and along the line of her jaw, mesmerising her with the intensity of his gaze. His touch forged a path of fire, created a breathlessness that robbed her of speech.

'Your skin is warm . . . soft as silk . . .'

His head descended, bringing his mouth to within an inch of her lips, his eyes claiming hers in a long, searching look from which she found it impossible to escape. His nearness overwhelmed her . . . threatened . . . promised . . .

Trapped, Jenna trembled in unbidden anticipation of the touch of his mouth on hers. It didn't come and she tried to turn her head away, but the hand which had been idly caressing her chin held her firm.

His mouth closed suddenly on hers, stifling the half-formed protest she tried to make. His lips were firm, but gentle, arousing an agony of sweetness she had never known. His expression of moments ago had led her to expect harshness—cruelty—instead, his mouth explored hers slowly, his tongue caressing the sweet inner contours of her yearning mouth. His fingers moved to her neckline, toying with the buttons he had just fastened.

The movement of his hand brought her briefly to her senses, her eyes flying open to meet the darkly smouldering gaze above her, but in the next instant his mouth had reclaimed hers once more, his kiss now demanding a response which she found it all too easy to give.

Her whole body shuddered as his cool fingers touched the sensitive under-curve of her breast and she tried to pull away—to control the feverish excitement which threatened to engulf her—but he fought the weak movement, imprisoning her with his mouth and his hands until she was forced to give up... to surrender with a ragged moan.

Then, with a sudden angry movement that had her heart jumping, he jerked away, staring down into her face as though it was *she* who had been trying to seduce *him*.

A slow trickle of humiliation became a flood and bright, angry tears stung her eyes.

'Why did you do that?' she demanded in a cracked whisper.

Their eyes met and held and Jenna was aware of a kaleidoscope of emotions, moving like windblown shadows across a landscape.

He touched her cheek with seeming tenderness. 'Poetic justice, perhaps.'

'For whom?'

But his mood had changed. He was moving away again, towards the window, leaving Jenna full of shame at her eager responses, humiliated by the ease with which her defences had crumbled before his deliberate assault.

'How you must hate my family,' she said dully. 'Is the Fergusson vengeance reserved only for helpless women?'

He turned and she saw that his face was pale.

'No. Not only for women.' He gave a bitter smile. 'And I have yet to meet a truly helpless woman.' His eyes fixed contemptuously on her gaping neckline, which revealed the rise and fall of her breasts with each ragged breath.

'Women have an armoury of very potent weapons.' His gaze raked her insinuatingly and Jenna's hand crept to her neckline, dragging the nightgown across her exposed breast. 'Fortunately for men, very few learn to use them to any very damaging effect.'

Jenna glared at him. 'Very few honest women would want to.'

'Is there such a thing?' He seemed to be asking the question of himself.

He shrugged, as though tired of the subject, and turned his attention once more to her neckline. 'Your buttons seem to need my attention again.' Coolly he reached out a hand.

'Don't you dare touch me.' Jenna slapped it away and shrank from him.

There was a dangerous glitter in his eyes. 'Don't dare me, my dear little wild thing. As you rightly point

out, you're defenceless, so make no empty threats.'
A sardonic smile deepened the cleft in his chin.
'Perhaps what you really want is for me to teach you
another lesson.'

Jenna stared at him.

'What I really want is for you to go,' she gritted.
'I would have thought even unwelcome guests warrant
some courtesy. Or is it a Scottish custom to treat all
female visitors as fair game?'

She was agreeably surprised by the deep flush which
ran beneath his skin. It told her it was possible to
penetrate even his tough arrogant skin.

'You're right, of course,' he said evenly. 'I'm be-
having very badly. A trait, it seems, you Andersons
have a knack of arousing in me.'

'My name is Wilde, not Anderson,' she reminded
him icily. 'I'm afraid I can't answer for my aunt or
my cousin, but, for my own part, I'll take care to
arouse no feelings of any kind in you.'

His eyebrows rose. His colour had returned to
normal, Jenna noted, and there was a faint cynical
curve to his mouth.

'I'd be interested to know how you propose to do
that.'

She flushed beneath his sombre mockery. 'By
avoiding your company completely in the future,
which, I can assure you, will be no hardship.'

'You surprise me,' he said sardonically, rubbing his
thumb and forefinger against his faintly shadowed
chin.

Jenna caught the subtle scent of his aftershave and
squirmed as she recalled her reactions to the sensation
of his cheek against hers and she could bear it no
longer.

He let his eyes wander over her body, outlined by the thin bedcover, and she burned with mortification. Lying here, she was at a disadvantage and he knew it.

'May I get out of bed?' she enquired sarcastically. 'I don't think I'll come to any harm. I've only hurt my wrist, you know. There's nothing wrong with my feet.'

She pulled back the bedcovers and swung her legs over the side of the bed.

'So I see,' he said laconically, his eyes fixed on her bare thighs, and he laughed as she tried to pull the nightgown down around them.

She pulled herself back into bed and replaced the bedcover.

'When you leave, I'll get up,' she said with dignity. 'Then, I'll take Suzie and, if necessary, we'll walk into Glenrae.'

'Barefoot and dressed in Annie's nightgown?' His deep laugh sounded amused. 'Dr McRae advised rest to give that wrist a chance to mend. Perhaps more importantly, he thinks there's a chance your young sister has concussion and only time will tell. So if you don't care for your own health, I think you should consider hers.'

'Concussion!' Jenna's face paled. 'Will she be all right?'

'I'm sure she will.' He touched a hand almost absently against her tousled hair. 'You've both had a bad shake-up, so why not be sensible and relax?'

'I want to see Suzie for myself. She's probably worrying and wondering where I am.'

'I assure you your sister's being well looked after and is perfectly happy. You can see her later.'

He pushed her back firmly. 'Annie will be along with your breakfast in a minute or two.' He gave a short ironic laugh. 'Lots of good porridge oats, if I'm not mistaken, to give you back your strength.'

Jenna sank back on to her pillows, her fighting spirit receding temporarily under his persistence. 'I'll eat a bucket of the stuff,' she muttered resentfully, 'if it will get me out of here.'

A sardonic expression crossed his rugged face. 'Then let's hope it does the trick.'

His words held a bitterness that didn't escape Jenna's sensitive heart. He didn't want her here—so why was he insisting that she stay? Was this some subtle kind of torture? Part of his revenge against her family?

To Jenna's relief, the bedroom door opened at that moment to admit his cook, bearing a loaded tray.

Duncan Fergusson's stern features relaxed into an unexpected smile.

'Here's Annie. With enough food to feed a hungry battalion by the looks of it.'

Unruffled by his teasing, Annie bustled towards the bed, her round blue eyes fixed on Jenna's face. 'How are ye feeling?'

'I feel fine.' Jenna shot Duncan Fergusson a sidelong glance, daring him to argue the point.

He was standing by watchfully, his hands negligently thrust into the pockets of his riding breeches. He looked fantastic, she conceded grudgingly. If you like the grim, determined type.

'And what are ye doing here?' Annie shot him a sharp look.

Duncan's eyes were on Jenna. 'I came to offer some assistance, but it wasn't received very kindly.' His gaze

slipped down to fix pointedly on her once more un-
buttoned neckline.

Jenna gasped and clutched the nightgown about her,
furious at the tell-tale flush which let him know he
had hit his mark.

'When you see fit to let me have my case, I can get
dressed in some of my own clothes.'

He stared at her coolly. 'Your luggage is still in your
car, I'm afraid. Last night I was too busy worrying
about your young sister to waste time with that. If I
have time later today, I'll go up there and get it.'

'You're so kind,' Jenna said tightly.

'I can be.' He raised a coolly mocking eyebrow. 'But
only in a worthy cause.'

'Which I'm not, I suppose,' she hissed furiously,
and then mentally kicked herself as she saw his thin
smile. Why did she take the bait so easily? 'I hate
you.'

'You won't be the first member of your family to
do that,' he replied with infuriating calm. 'I'll try not
to let it worry me.'

The mocking light left his eyes and he turned
sharply away.

'Our guest is Louise Anderson's niece,' he told
Annie, sounding suddenly strained. 'She'll be staying
until she's better. Make her welcome.'

Annie looked stunned, her round head moving from
side to side in apparent disbelief. He seemed satisfied
with her silent reaction. In the doorway, he cast a final
glance over his shoulder at Jenna.

'If you *really* want to leave, you'll eat well and get
your strength up.'

Jenna suspected the emphasis he placed on the word
'really' was a deliberate insult, meant to remind her

that he'd understood the effect he'd had on her, and it filled her with impotent fury.

'Annie,' she said fretfully, when he'd left, 'what is the matter with that man? Why does he hate the Andersons so much?'

Annie shrugged. 'It's not for me to say.' She lifted Jenna forward and plumped up the pillows behind her. 'Like Master Duncan said—ye've got to eat.'

'All I want is to get on to Glenrae.' Jenna's face set grimly. 'And when I do, I hope I never have to set eyes on Duncan Fergusson ever again.'

There was a mysterious smile playing about Annie's full lips.

'Glenrae's a small place, m'dearie. Here, no one can help but bump into their neighbours . . . sooner or later.'

CHAPTER THREE

JENNA was sitting at the window in a large armchair, where she could look out at the view. It was breathtaking.

The garden had the natural unrestrained look of parkland and stretched into the distance. From her window, she could see that the house occupied quite a high position. Beyond the garden, a rolling sweep of land dipped down to a valley, where a silver-bright river meandered, snake-like, into a far-distant gap between two jutting ridges.

Last night the Scottish countryside had seemed bleak, but today, in the clear light of an exquisitely sunny day, the landscape was anything but bleak and filled Jenna with a strange aching sensation which was hard to describe, but which fired her imagination.

It wasn't hard to understand why the Scots were so proud of their homeland. The mountains, blue and hazy in the distance, were an enchanting backdrop to the wild, extravagant purple-green sweep of the valley, and emanated a power which seemed to hint at shrouded secrets of a tumultuous past.

She'd seen nothing of Duncan Fergusson since the button-fastening incident of the morning. Despite his insistence that she stay, he hadn't bothered to come and check on her progress. It annoyed her to realise that he took her obedience for granted, but it wasn't really surprising, since there was nothing else she could do, when she felt so weak.

But her weakness hadn't deterred her from walking along the landing to see Suzie. She bit her lip at the sight of her sister's pale little face and the bruises showing around the dressing on her temple.

'Are you sure she's all right?' Jenna asked the rosy-cheeked young woman who was sitting beside Suzie's bed, reading from a book of fables.

'Well, if her appetite's anything to go on, she's fine.'

Jenna gave a rueful smile. Despite her thin frame, her sister's capacity for food had always been a source of wonder. If she was still eating well, there couldn't be a lot wrong.

'How are you doing, pet?' she asked, kissing the pale cheek.

'I'm OK,' Suzie said stoically. 'And when I'm really better, Duncan's going to take me down to the stables,' she beamed enthusiastically.

Jenna's eyes widened in surprise at Suzie's easy use of their host's name.

'Well, that's nice of him,' she responded, feeling genuinely touched at this evidence of his kindness to her sister. Obviously, his animosity didn't extend to children, even those related to the Andersons, and that had to be a point in his favour.

'He brought Alex up to meet me. Alex has red hair and works in the stables. He says if I hurry up and get really better I can ride Bella. She's the best-tempered horse in the stables.'

As she padded back to her own room, she mused that Duncan Fergusson seemed to have found a way of keeping Suzie happily lying in her bed. Did he imagine he had achieved the same with Jenna? Hardly. Even he couldn't believe she'd be content to remain cooped up indoors for hours on end ... imprisoned in an over-large nightdress.

Her enquiry later as to the whereabouts of her cases brought a shrug from Annie and the blunt reply that Master Duncan was taking care of all that.

The woman was obviously devoted to her employer and Jenna sensed it would do no good to try and coax her into bringing her clothes.

Duncan Fergusson would pay for this, she vowed grimly. When he came, she would ... But he didn't come. Annie came with her lunch, but would answer no questions, and by the middle of the afternoon Jenna was ready to commit murder. She'd got up to look out of the window, hoping to distract herself from her brooding anger and, for a while, the beautiful view had had a tranquillising effect on her. But as time ticked slowly by she again grew agitated.

Somewhere, dogs were barking, and she longed to be out of doors.

Leaning out from the window, she caught a glimpse of a paved terrace, close to the house. A flash of white moved gently in the light breeze, where a table was laid for tea. Oh, what she wouldn't give for a breath of fresh air and a nice cup of tea.

Anger at her internment returned and, with a surge of determination, she crossed to the door of her room and went out into the corridor. Outside, she hesitated, looking down at the voluminous nightgown which hung in folds about her feet. Hardly suitable wear to be traipsing about someone else's house in the middle of the afternoon.

She was almost tempted to turn back and wait until Annie came up with her tea, but decided against it. After all, it wasn't her fault she had no clothes to

wear. Her state of undress was part of Duncan
Fergusson's plan to keep her prisoner in her room and
she wasn't going to let him get away with it any longer.
She would go and find Annie and demand access to
her cases and some of her own clothes.

After only a slight hesitation, she set off along the
corridor, noting wryly that it was more of an art
gallery than a corridor, with family portraits hung the
length of the wall facing the tall windows.

The bearded and bewhiskered faces of Duncan
Fergusson's male ancestors gazed sternly down at her.
And a tough-looking bunch they were too. There was
only one female and even she had a hardness of eye
that was intimidating.

The thick, red-patterned carpet fell a foot short each
side of the heavy skirtings, disclosing borders of
gleaming oak floorboards. Above was a fine dark-
timbered ceiling and Jenna realised that the house
must be very old. It probably had lots of surprising
nooks and crannies which she would have loved to
explore and she couldn't help a little feeling of disappointment that she wouldn't be around long enough
to do so.

At the end of the corridor, close to the head of the
stairs, a heavy door hung open to disclose an intriguing semi-circular room which seemed part of
some kind of tower construction. Its walls were lined
with uniquely curved bookshelves, supported by in-
tricately carved wooden brackets.

The room was empty and, unable to restrain her
curiosity, she went in, her hand running appreciat-
ively across the smooth surfaces of the carved wooden
desk and the cool leather of the chairs.

'Looking for something?' The drily accented voice startled Jenna.

He was so close behind her that she could feel his warm breath against her ear. She turned awkwardly, her knees buckling with sudden weakness.

'Sit down, before you fall down.'

He indicated one of the leather chairs and Jenna sat reluctantly, watching him as he lowered his tall frame into a chair opposite. She was relieved. If he'd remained standing she would have been at a disadvantage, forced to look up into his cool, rugged face.

'Were you searching for something in particular?'

His implication of prying was a deliberate provocation, she knew, and she struggled to keep her voice calm as she answered.

'No. I was just admiring your house. I find it fascinating.'

He grunted. 'Perhaps you'd find it less so if you had to live in it.'

She shook her head. 'I don't think so. I love old houses with their thick walls and secret places. This house has history. I mean . . . people have really lived here for centuries. I hate the modern box Suzie and I live in at the moment . . .'

Jenna caught herself up. She'd been rambling from a mixture of nerves and enthusiasm and wondered how much she had revealed of her longing for past roots.

It was hard to gauge his reaction, but for a brief moment, his eyes held hers with a probing intensity which appeared, for once, to be without rancour.

'Well. Since you like it so much,' he said slowly, 'one day perhaps, when you're feeling better, you might like to see over it properly.'

Jenna blinked. Was that a promise or just a polite rejoinder? 'Thank you. I'd like that.'

He stood up and reached out to help her to her feet. She rose, feeling the warmth of his hand through the cumbersome material of her gown. The sensations his touch aroused were unfamiliar and distracting.

'But for now,' he went on, 'perhaps you should give up exploring and go back to bed.'

Jenna's clear violet eyes flew to his, filled with frustration. 'I'm sick of bed. I'm not an invalid and I won't let you go on pretending that I am.'

'Pretending? What an odd thing to say.' His eyes narrowed. 'I'm simply trying to make sure you follow Dr McRae's advice and rest for a couple of days after your shake-up.'

'Well, thank you for your concern,' she replied a little caustically. 'But I've had more than enough rest for now and I am on my way downstairs for tea . . . hopefully out of doors.'

He stood back to look at her, one eyebrow raised in cool mockery. 'Dressed like that?'

Following his raking glance, Jenna saw that, despite the fastened buttons, the loose neckline still revealed too much of her cleavage and the prominent evidence of her unwilling response to him.

'It's your fault I'm dressed this way,' she replied furiously. 'And I insist you let me have my case, and free access to my own clothes.'

He studied her furious face with deliberate intentness.

'I suppose the temper comes from the hint of red in your hair.'

He was turning on the charm, knowing he had the power to melt her resistance. She caught his glance flicking once more to her breasts.

In a surge of frustrated anger, she lashed out at his face with her good hand. He captured her wrist easily, holding it lightly but firmly, sending her pulse racing. She fumed helplessly as he drew her hand to his lips for a brief kiss.

'I can't make up my mind when you look your loveliest,' he jeered softly. 'Pale and frightened ... or red with rage, as you are at the moment.'

'Callous...despicable...' she ranted, and he laughed coldly, drawing her into his arms, despite her struggles. 'Coward! To take advantage of——'

'A helpless female!' He finished her sentence for her and then, without warning, dipped his head to cover her protesting mouth with his, stemming her angry retort with a deep kiss, slowly, inexorably moulding her unwilling body to his.

Jenna pushed her hands angrily against his chest, distracted suddenly by the powerful beat of his heart beneath her fingers, astonished to find that it had accelerated alarmingly. So, she thought exultantly, he wasn't as cool and controlled as he pretended to be. He was as strongly affected by the kiss as she was.

With slow deliberation, she softened her lips on his, allowing her body to melt against him, noting with satisfaction the pause and resurgent momentum of his heart. Pure elation sped through her. She wasn't as completely helpless against him as she'd thought. She had the power to move him.

It was he who drew apart eventually, thrusting her gently away, and Jenna could see the burning glow of his eyes and the narrowing of his nostrils as he fought to steady his breathing.

'I couldn't let you go on maligning me,' he said, sounding oddly unsteady. 'I had to save you from yourself.'

'Do you always need to find a reason for kissing me?' She eyed him challengingly. 'Are you afraid I might think you enjoy it?'

She knew he was no man to play with, but allowed herself her moment of triumph. His face darkened. It seemed, for a moment, as though he would seize her again, but instead he moved back from her, thrusting his hands deep into the pockets of his breeches and surveying her coolly.

'Sharp as well as beautiful.'

'Don't patronise me, Mr Fergusson,' she said tightly.

He shrugged. 'That was patronising, was it? I thought it was merely observant.' His mouth curled in a sardonic smile.

'Charm might work with Suzie,' she said cuttingly. 'But you won't find me so easy to overcome.'

'I hope not.' He looked amused. 'Where's the sport in easy prey?'

Jenna gasped, her eyes widening indignantly. 'Prey runs, Mr Fergusson, making you into the hunter. When it turns and faces you, capable of attack, it becomes an adversary. What do you do then?'

He frowned, seeming to consider the question seriously for a few seconds. 'That's a tricky one,' he said at last, then he shrugged. 'I suppose I'd shoot it just the same.'

He was watching her closely, a gleam of what might be humour lurking in his dark eyes, which Jenna deliberately ignored. If it was meant to be a joke, she refused to see the funny side of it.

'I think you would too.' She drew herself up regally. 'I'll go back to my room to wait and I'd be glad if you'd arrange for my case to be brought up right away.'

He answered her cool stare with an enigmatic look and as she saw the mocking glint in his eyes, she allowed her temper to flare.

'And if I'm not in possession of my own clothes within the next ten minutes, I might well appear for tea on the terrace stark naked.'

He burst into amused laughter, which had her grinding her teeth in rage.

'A situation I will most definitely enjoy.'

She eyed him icily. 'But not one my relatives will enjoy hearing about when I finally get to Glenrae.'

His face hardened. 'Am I intended to find that remark intimidating?'

Jenna brushed a hand over her dishevelled hair, feeling suddenly tired to death of the struggle to win over him.

She turned from him. 'Frankly, Mr Fergusson, I don't give a damn one way or the other.'

He laughed. 'I think you'll find that's my line, Miss O'Hara, or may I call you Scarlett?'

Jenna spun around to face him hotly, feeling a little foolish and wishing she'd chosen her words more carefully.

'I don't give a damn about that either. I'm sick of whatever game it is you're playing.' She gritted her teeth. 'Just find my clothes.'

'I'll do my best.' He spread his hands in a defeated gesture which didn't fool her for a moment. 'Meanwhile, I'll tell Annie to expect you for tea.'

Jenna heard voices as she descended the stairs into the hall. She followed the sound, which led her through a large, attractive sitting-room, bright and airy in the light from the two tall French windows.

Annie had come up to her bedroom, closely followed by a carrot-headed lad carrying Jenna's case.

'Put it down there, Alex,' Annie had commanded, pointing to the bottom of the bed.

He'd obeyed silently and Jenna had looked at him with interest. So this was Suzie's new friend from the stables. He gave her a bashful grin before leaving.

'I'll wait tea for ye,' Annie said. 'But don't be too long.'

Jenna had chosen a loose cotton frock in shades of violet which matched her eyes and brushed her hair until it gleamed. She took care with her light make-up, wanting Duncan Fergusson to see her as far removed as possible from the waif he'd brought home with him the night before.

Still following the voices, she was led outside. She recognised Duncan's deep tones but wondered at the light musical female voice which interspersed with his, hesitating as a tight feeling of apprehension caught her unawares. Was there a female member of his family? Mother? Wife? For some reason, it was something she hadn't considered. She was tempted to retreat, but forced herself to go on, stepping determinedly out on to the wide stone-paved terrace.

Both speakers turned towards her, Duncan's expression remote, the girl's frankly speculative. Jenna

noted this uneasily, along with the heart-shaped beauty
of the girl's face, framed by vibrant dark auburn hair.
Her skin was lightly tanned, with an attractive dusting
of freckles across the bridge of her finely chiselled
nose. But her most startling feature was her large yel-
lowish-green eyes, which swept up at the outer edges
to give her a striking feline appearance.

'Ah! Miss Wilde.' Duncan rose to his feet and held
out a chair. As she sat, he went on. 'Meet Marianne
Tyson. You'll be seeing a lot of each other, I imagine,
since she's your cousin's partner in the riding school.'

'Oh!' It was impossible not to show surprise. So,
not everyone connected with the Andersons was a
victim of his vindictiveness.

She looked at the girl with veiled curiosity. No one
had told her Stuart had a partner, but, even if they
had, she could never have imagined this elegant
creature sprawled in the wrought-iron chair.

Marianne's strange eyes raked her from head to
foot, her full mouth curving in a disconcerting smile
which made her look even more like a cat.

'So, this is dear Cousin Jenna,' she drawled lazily.
'Louise was worried, but I'm sure you're taking good
care of her.'

Duncan looked amused. 'Your claws are showing,
Marianne.'

'Nonsense.' Marianne's smile showed perfect teeth.
'I'm here to offer the hand of friendship.' She turned
her attention to Jenna, but she didn't hold out her
hand. 'I'm sure you must be longing to see your aunt.
I'll be perfectly happy to take you on to the school if
you're well enough to leave.'

Before Jenna had a chance to reply, Duncan interrupted. 'As I've already explained to you, Marianne,

that won't be necessary. Jenna will stay until Dr McRae calls again, which will be tomorrow. We'll see what he says.'

'Suit yourself.' Marianne's elegant shoulders rose in a shrug and her green eyes narrowed on Jenna's face, which was flushed with anger.

Duncan Fergusson had no right to answer for her in that high-handed way, and she had to bite her lip to keep from telling him so in front of his visitor.

'I think you might be allowed to keep your little prize a while longer,' Marianne went on silkily, her expression saying clearly that she couldn't understand why he should want Jenna there. 'Since it obviously means such a lot to you.' She gave a grim little laugh. 'But don't leave it too late. Stuart might get impatient. He's been eagerly awaiting his cousin's arrival also.'

'Marianne,' Duncan growled warningly, 'I've warned you before about stirring the cauldron.'

She retreated into laughter, raising slim hands in mock defence. 'Oh, peace, darling,' she cried prettily. 'You know what I'm like.'

'Only too well,' he said grimly. 'But, one day, you'll go too far.'

Marianne didn't seem to mind his irritable temper and some instinct warned Jenna that these two might be more than just close neighbours.

Marianne shrugged. 'I'm serious, darling. Louise Anderson has plans for Cousin Jenna. Though I hardly think she's Stuart's type.' Her gaze swept critically over Jenna. 'Nor yours either, for that matter.'

'Since when are you an authority on that subject?' Duncan's face fired with colour. 'And you can spare me the fairy stories.'

She laughed. 'Very well. If you don't want to know what Louise has in mind, I won't tell you.'

'I can guess.' He glowered. 'Louise always was a blind fool where he's concerned, despite the fact he's not her own blood. It would have been better if she'd let him go, instead of...' He paused and drove his fist into his palm in sudden fury. 'Damn him! As long as he's still here to remind me...'

Marianne touched his hand, all teasing gone. 'It was an accident, Duncan. Perhaps it's time you buried the past. You can't go on living with a ghost forever.'

'I'll live whichever way I choose.' He shook her away and stood up abruptly. 'Didn't you say you were in a hurry to leave?'

He turned and walked away and Marianne got up to follow him, leaving Jenna to wonder what it had all been about.

Annie came with the tea trolley, surprised to find Jenna sitting alone.

'Is Master Duncan not having his tea?'

'I don't know.'

Jenna sat on, toying with the food on her plate, her mind on the scene she had just witnessed, trying to make some sense out of what had been said. At last, she gave up the pretence of eating and got up. She was suddenly weary and her room, with its comfortable bed, seemed surprisingly like a haven.

In the hall, Jenna froze and moved back into a shadowed corner. Duncan was there with Marianne. He had his back to her, but Marianne's face was in clear view, lifted to his, her eyes smiling seductively.

Duncan's hands were lying loosely on her waist, seeming to deny passion, but Marianne moved closer, wrapping her arms tightly about his neck, pressing her voluptuous body to him and offering her lips. He hesitated for a moment and then bent his head to kiss her.

Neither noticed Jenna as she passed quickly by and ascended the stairs.

Back in her room, she lay across the bed, staring up at the high ceiling above, her eyes blindly tracing the elaborate lines of the cornice in an attempt to blot out her angry thoughts. An hour ago, it had been she who had been in his arms, elated because she'd felt the surging beat of his heart and imagined she'd stirred an unusual response in him. Now, he was in Marianne's arms and it was she who was feeling the excited thud of his heartbeats. So, she'd been right in guessing they were lovers.

It was obvious that he was a man who found it easy to respond to a woman . . . a man aware also of his own power to arouse, and it seemed he had no qualms about using it to his own ends.

He must have felt Jenna's response to his love-making . . . an illusion of tenderness . . . a deliberate campaign of revenge. But for what? She needed to know, but in this house there was no one who would relieve the frustration of her ignorance. Would there be anyone at Glenrae?

Jenna groaned and turned on her stomach. It was possible she might never know what had happened between Duncan Fergusson and her cousin Stuart Anderson. Once away from this house, it might no longer matter, she reasoned forlornly. Despite Annie's conviction that Jenna would meet with Duncan Fergusson again, it was unlikely that he would seek her out to continue his revenge, and she would certainly be doing her best to avoid him. The thought should have made her feel better, but instead it left her aching and hollow.

Annie came up later with an invitation from Duncan for Jenna to have dinner with him. She refused, giving the excuse of a headache, and then had to suffer the pangs of guilt as Annie fussed about her, worried that it might be the result of the accident. She hated herself for the lie, wishing she could set Annie's mind at rest, but was relieved not to have to face Duncan again.

But relief turned to loneliness when, with Suzie fast asleep, the evening stretched ahead quiet and empty.

Annie had obviously passed on her excuse to Duncan, and yet he hadn't even bothered to check whether she was all right. She could have had a relapse and died of shock for all he cared, she thought with wry anger.

At last, Annie came up with a nightcap and further incensed Jenna by telling her that Duncan had gone out to dinner rather than eat alone. She wondered if he'd gone to Marianne.

She lay awake for hours, turning everything over in her mind, wondering what her aunt was making of Jenna's predicament. Surely she must be concerned.

Marianne had probably been her aunt's advocate, sent to find out how Jenna was, since the enmity that existed between the families seemed to preclude the direct approach, and Jenna wondered what her aunt would make of Duncan's refusal to let her go.

Jenna groaned. It was possible her aunt was already regretting her impulse in inviting her two nieces up to Scotland for the summer. In which case, she might be perfectly happy for Duncan to keep them.

Louise Anderson hadn't seen Jenna since she was a girl and she'd never even met Suzie. Her aunt was sister to Jenna's mother and when both Jenna's parents had died in a tragic boating accident a year ago she had written of her regret at not being able to attend the funeral due to a bad fall from a horse resulting in broken bones. Jenna had written back and they'd kept in touch.

It had been a difficult year. Suzie had been devastated by the loss of her parents and Jenna, left in sole charge of a six-year-old sister, had found it hard to combine her own grief with the need to earn a living for them both. As she had been a teacher in a local primary school, it had made things a little easier to be home the same time as Suzie, but money had been very tight and there was no possibility of managing a holiday away from home.

And then, like a bolt of lightning from the blue, had come the loss of her job. The head had been sympathetic, but there had been nothing she could do. Finances had dictated the loss of one teacher, and, since Jenna had been the youngest and the last in, she had been the obvious one out.

Louise's letter, asking whether they would like to spend the summer at Glenrae, helping out in her stepson's riding school, had seemed like the answer to a prayer. It provided a respite in which to earn their keep and a change of scenery for Suzie, keeping her active and happy for the long school holidays.

Before leaving for Scotland, she'd sent out letters of application for jobs, but it was unlikely she'd receive any replies until term began again.

If she was honest, she hadn't wanted to miss the opportunity of paying a visit to her only living relatives.

Jenna had never met Stuart Anderson. Her aunt Louise had been widowed quite young and eight years ago had married a widower with a teenage son and gone to live up in Scotland. She'd kept in touch with her sister Margaret, Jenna's mother, but had never come back again to visit her home town.

Her description of Stuart Anderson had been glowing and it was obvious she'd regarded him as her own ever since her marriage. Now she was a widow again and all that Duncan and Marianne had said implied she now devoted her life and energies to her stepson, a fact that obviously filled Duncan Fergusson with resentment.

She sighed again, wondering what the outcome of this current situation would be. Would it lead to a stirring up of even greater bitterness between the two families? She fervently hoped not.

It was pointless to conjecture, of course. Nevertheless, she seemed unable to discontinue the endless round of fruitless thought.

CHAPTER FOUR

THE clock at Jenna's bedside said two o'clock and she was still awake. She sighed. It seemed that a book from the library was the only solution to her problem, and she slipped out of bed to find her robe.

Quietly, she moved along the corridor, only to find that the library door was locked.

She stood irresolute, trying to decide whether she would put on some outdoor clothes and take a stroll in the garden, when she noticed the turret staircase set in a corner opposite. Her eyes were drawn to the intricate wrought-iron handrail and she counted five steps before the circular stone column hid the rest from sight. Intrigued, and unable to resist the temptation to explore, she crossed and began, a little hesitantly, to ascend.

A small lead-paned window shed moonlight in a faint blue glow as she rounded the column. At the top of the stairway was a narrow corridor. One oval roof-light was all there was to relieve the darkness, and the doors off the corridor were tightly shut.

Crossing slowly to the nearest door, she opened it, brushing her hand along the inside wall to locate the light switch. The room was small, its walls lined with cupboards from floor to ceiling, and, in one corner, was a narrow wash-hand basin beneath a round bevelled mirror.

Unable to resist the temptation to explore further, she opened the door to another room which led off, and snapped on the light. The room held a single bed made up with floral bedlinen. The furniture was tastefully beautiful and the carpet was a deep soft pink, luxurious underfoot. All obviously chosen with a great deal of care and love. With its nursery pictures on the wall, it seemed like a room for a child. A child past or future? she wondered.

Feeling suddenly like an intruder, she turned to leave. As she did so, something heavy descended on her shoulder, startling her into a scream which was immediately stifled by a large hand.

Granite-hard almost black eyes glared into her terrified violet ones. For a moment, she could hardly recognise the savage face that loomed above hers. Duncan Fergusson took his hand from her mouth slowly and stood back.

'What are you doing up here?'

Jenna's body shook with nervous reaction. 'You...you frightened me.' Her heart pumped unevenly. 'Did you have to creep up on me like that?'

He gave an impatient snort. 'I came up here expecting to find a burglar. Do you imagine I'd advertise my presence?' The ice-cold look he gave her was intimidating. 'Do you often prowl about people's homes in the early hours?'

'Of course not.' Jenna snapped irritably. 'I couldn't sleep. I got up to find a book.'

He laughed grimly. 'The library is on the floor below. You were there this afternoon...remember?'

She felt tempted to lower her head, but resisted the impulse, and forced herself to look resolutely into his strangely hostile eyes.

'It was locked,' she said, as reasonably as she could manage. 'Then I saw that intriguing circular staircase and wondered where it led.' She tossed her head with a return of defiance. 'I wasn't aware curiosity was a crime.'

His body tensed angrily and she was suddenly conscious that he wore only pyjamas. Her eyes riveted on the rippling torso apparent through the thin silky material and her heart beat in erratic response to the sight.

'Well, now you know,' he said coldly. 'Is your curiosity satisfied.'

'No. Not really.'

He was angry and it was madness to go on, but Jenna felt something in her bones and had to know. 'Has this room anything to do with your feud with my cousin?'

He stood still for a moment then took a step towards her, and Jenna noted the pallor of his face. It reminded her of the way he'd looked that first time she'd seen him, peering in at her through the car window.

'I think you've pried enough for one night,' he gritted. 'If you don't mind, I'd like to get some sleep.'

'Same here,' Jenna answered defiantly, but unable to hide the tide of colour which rose to her face. Wasn't it natural she should want to probe the mystery which was causing her so much discomfort. He didn't have to be so nasty, did he? 'If I could have got off to sleep, I wouldn't be here, giving you another opportunity to vent your spite on me.'

'Spite!' he repeated, giving her a hard glare. 'This is no matter of childish spite——'

'Then what is it? I'd really like to know.'

She saw a look of what seemed like pain sweep across his rugged face and her voice softened.

'Perhaps, if you told me, I could understand.' Without thinking, she put her hand gently on his arm. 'It might even help to talk about it.'

For a moment, their eyes met ... hers appealing, his hard and probing ... and then he grabbed her roughly into his arms, his mouth descending on hers in a crushing kiss that bruised her lips and sent a flame searing through her, that was as much excitement as resentment. But as his lips continued to plunder hers, the movement of his mouth against hers changed, deepening into an intimate exploration that had Jenna tingling with sensations she had never felt in her life before.

Involuntarily, her arms slid around him, her fingers burning with the feel of his hard body through the thin silky material. Despite herself, she moaned, pressing herself against him. He made an answering sound and moved his hand through her hair, tenderly caressing her scalp.

It seemed that the tension was leaving him, as he moulded her body to his but then he lifted his mouth from hers and gave a low, bitter laugh that had the passion draining away from her.

'Now what are you offering me, my little wild thing?' He asked mockingly. 'Your sweet body as sacrificial lamb?'

A cold finger of ice crept up Jenna's spine as she looked into his darkly gleaming eyes. She said thinly, 'Don't be ridiculous. Why on earth should I sacrifice myself?'

'You tell me.'

'This is nonsense.' The worst of it was, she didn't know why she'd allowed herself to respond to him in

that abandoned way. It had never happened before
with any other man . . . not even Martin . . .

'Perhaps I felt sorry——'

'You felt pity . . . for me?' he exclaimed fiercely, his
dark eyes burning into hers. His large hand crept beneath the fall of her hair to the nape of her neck,
imprisoning her. 'That's not what I want from you.'

His fingers bit into Jenna's skin.

'Then let me go!' she cried. 'Because I certainly
feel nothing else for you.'

He made a mocking sound. 'You're lying, and we
both know it.'

Colour flooded her face. He was right. Just because she couldn't label the feelings, it didn't mean
they didn't exist. She was filled with a mixture of humiliation and a hopeless longing for him to understand what she couldn't yet understand herself.

She panicked as his head began to lower. If he kissed
her again . . .

'Go to hell!' she cried raggedly.

Gathering her strength, she tore herself from him
and fled the room, rushing through the dressing-room
and on to the dark landing, seeing little through the
blur of unaccountable tears, feeling little as her bare
feet struck against the metal at the top of the staircase.
Some instinct for survival sent her sprawling backwards rather than forwards into the dark tumbling
chasm of the stairwell.

He caught her before she reached the ground, his
arms closing swiftly about her to swing her up to
safety.

Trembling with shock, she clung to him, her head
pressed into his shoulder, where her cheek felt the
frightened hammering of his heart.

'You little idiot,' he said harshly. 'You might have broken your neck.'

Jenna lifted her head to look at him accusingly. 'Isn't that what you want? An eye for an eye?'

He put her from him and she saw the planes of his face harden in the faint glimmer of the moon. 'Is that what you believe?'

'Yes.' There was no compromise in her affirmation.

He stared into her eyes and an inexplicable spark glowed between them, a fraction of a second when, defences lowered, they met on some hitherto unattainable equal ground, and she felt an irrational hope.

She watched the frown form between his brows . . . change his expression . . . and knew that, whatever it was she had seen, it was gone.

'It's getting late,' he said at last. 'And I have to be away early in the morning.' He took her elbow. 'I'll see you back to your room.'

She shook herself free. 'You don't have to. Whatever secret you're guarding is safe for now. You have my word I won't be doing any more exploring tonight.'

She moved quickly away from him, down the spiral staircase. Half expecting him to follow, she turned on the last step to glance upward and behind, seeing nothing but the blue, eerie glow of the moon reflecting on the smooth rounded wall.

For a long time, Duncan stood at the head of the stairs, hearing the muted patter of her bare feet and then the heavy silence left behind.

He could still feel the sensations of her small, soft body in his embrace, the frightened pressure of her arms about his neck, her face touching softly against the base of his throat. Her near fall had shaken them both and her trembling had awakened in him a fierce, surging protectiveness. Emotions long buried ran riot through his tall frame. Feelings that had lost nothing of their power for having lain dormant for so long.

Jenna was up early, despite her disturbed night. Duncan Fergusson's behaviour the night before seemed to confirm her suspicions that he was out for some kind of revenge. And for that, of course, it was easier if she was close to hand.

She felt angry. Now she understood his reasons for wanting her to stay, she determined to leave at the first opportunity. He had told her he would be away in the early part of the morning, so she hadn't expected to see him until later in the day. It was a surprise when, after a brief knock on her bedroom door, he entered.

'I hope I didn't wake you?' he said formally, his dark eyes flicking over her face.

'You didn't,' Jenna answered shortly.

She'd been sitting since dawn in the armchair in the window and he crossed to her, putting a cool hand beneath her chin, lifting her face to his, making it impossible for her to avoid his eyes and their shrewd appraisal.

'You look tired.'

'That's hardly surprising.' Jenna pulled away, stifling a flood of feeling at his touch.

'If you're implying it's my fault you're half dead with fatigue this morning, I'm afraid I can't follow your reasoning.'

'Can't you?' She flicked a scornful glance at him. 'Your behaviour last night was hardly conducive to restful sleep.'

He snorted. 'And would you say yours was? Have you always been a night prowler?'

Jenna flushed crimson. 'No. But if you shroud everything with secrecy, you can't blame me for trying to find my own answers.'

He regarded her with one dark brow raised. 'And did you find any?'

'None that make sense,' she snapped. 'But I'm glad you came, as I wanted to remind you—after Dr McRae's visit this morning, I want to leave.'

He stood back to survey her faintly flushed face.

'Indeed, that's why I came. To tell you Dr McRae won't be here today. There's a premature birth in the village and I'm afraid the lady in question takes priority.'

'Of course. Just what I might have expected, another delay.' Jenna eyed him coldly. 'Not that it matters. Waiting for him here is nonsense anyway. I'm perfectly fit and I'm sure Suzie's up to a short trip, but if he really thinks it necessary for us to have a check-up then he can call at the riding school.' She stood up. 'In fact, if Suzie's had her breakfast, I'd like you to take us immediately.'

'I'm sorry,' he said stiffly. 'But I'm afraid that's not possible. I have some urgent business to attend to which will probably take all day.'

'This is ridiculous.' Jenna made an exasperated sound. 'If my car was repaired I could drive myself without putting you to any further trouble.'

'Well, it isn't. It's in the local garage and it will be a week before it's back to normal.'

Jenna knew she should be grateful for that thoughtfulness at least, but somehow it was impossible to see it that way.

'Do be sensible,' he went on. 'It won't hurt you to wait another day. Suzie's up and about in the grounds this morning . . . enjoying her stay. Why can't you?'

His tone was that of an adult dealing with a difficult child and Jenna's blood boiled. But it seemed that, for the moment, there wasn't much she could do about it.

He waited for her answer and, when none was forthcoming, he nodded his satisfaction.

'If you feel like taking a walk, don't go any further than the stables. The pathway down to the lower orchard is rather rough and there's a very steep drop beyond the far stone wall.'

'How thoughtful of you to tell me,' Jenna said, with heavy irony. Did he think she didn't realise he was outlining the boundaries beyond which he wouldn't allow her to go?

'Hm,' he said almost absently. 'If you were staying longer, I'd show you the stables. I'm proud of my horses. Do you ride, by the way?'

'Of course. I wouldn't be much use to a riding school if I didn't.' She laughed cynically. 'But don't worry, I won't be making my escape that way. Suzie's a novice and I couldn't risk her on a strange horse.'

'Escape?' He frowned. 'Do you consider yourself a prisoner here?'

She snorted inelegantly. 'Well, I do seem to be having a bit of trouble getting away.'

His eyes glinted. 'I'm sorry. I didn't realise how much you wanted to see your aunt.' His mouth thinned, lifting contemptuously at one corner. 'Or is it your cousin you are longing to see?'

Jenna flushed angrily. 'Whichever it is ... it's none of your business.'

'Perhaps not.' His voice was clipped. 'Well, if you're that anxious to leave, then of course you must. But I really do have something important to take care of today. If you can be patient for one more day, I will take you tomorrow, I promise.'

His expression was withdrawn, dismissive.

Jenna flushed. In normal circumstances, she would have been grateful to him for his opportune rescue of herself and Suzie; she would have been admiring him for his thoughtfulness in arranging for the repair of her car; thanking him for the hospitality of his lovely house. But circumstances weren't normal and, in spite of everything, she would have to continue to regard him as her enemy.

'In the circumstances, I suppose I have no alternative,' she said at last.

He smiled sardonically. 'You're very gracious.' His mockery deepened her colour, but she said nothing.

'Will I see you at dinner tonight?' he asked unexpectedly. 'Or do you imagine I might try to drug you to keep you here against your will?'

'Don't be absurd.' Jenna frowned irritably.

'I'm glad there are some things you don't think I'm capable of.'

He grinned fleetingly, making him look younger and even more handsome, Jenna noted with a flare of interest, quickly doused. Whatever happened, she mustn't be tempted to lower her guard.

He was moving away, towards the door and paused to look back. 'Does that mean I *shall* see you at dinner...or will you have another of your headaches?'

Something in his mocking smile accused her of being afraid.

Jenna tossed her head back proudly. A headache the strength of ten wouldn't keep her away now. 'Thank you for your kind invitation. I'll be there.'

Later, when he'd gone, Jenna took a walk in the garden, wandering down to the stables, where she found Suzie, quite at home, mucking out.

'Good heavens, Suzie! Are you sure you're well enough for this?'

She knelt and drew the little girl towards her, gently touching the bruised swelling. It seemed to have receded a bit.

'I don't think you should overdo things just yet.'

'I won't, I promise.' Suzie beamed. 'I'm helping Alex.'

The carrot-haired lad came striding across the yard, carrying a number of feed bags slung across his shoulders. He nodded to Jenna.

'I'll finish that,' he told Suzie. 'You distribute these bags and then take a barrow down to the orchard and collect up the sound apples.'

Suzie glowed with pride. 'Alex is in charge and I'm his assistant.'

'Not a bad one either.' Alex ruffled Suzie's blonde curls and winked at Jenna. 'Master Duncan thought this would keep her out of mischief.'

Jenna looked a bit doubtful. 'Don't let her overdo it, will you?' she said in an aside.

He nodded his understanding and said quietly, 'Don't worry, I won't.'

'Duncan said I can ride Bella any time I like,' Suzie cut in. 'But I must learn to ride properly before I can go without the leading rein.' Her round blue eyes grew dreamy. 'I like Duncan so much.'

Jenna's expression softened and she ruffled Suzie's hair. 'I bet he'd be glad to know somebody does.'

Suzie frowned. 'Why? Don't you?'

'I can take him or leave him,' she said in a teasing voice. 'But he obviously likes little blondes best.'

Or, at least, they didn't come into his plans for revenge at the moment.

He didn't seem to be going out of his way to win *her* friendship, Jenna thought ruefully. In fact, just the opposite.

Her thoughts of his revenge had been hazy, perhaps a nebulous desire to hit back at Stuart Anderson. Now she was forced to ask herself what form she thought it would take, and she was at a loss. What was it he was hoping would happen? That if she stayed long enough she would fall in love with him? And, if so, why?

Jenna shook her head. The whole idea was preposterous. He had no guarantee she would fall in love.

And yet he was a powerful, charismatic man, her inner voice argued. Surely he must know that there were few women who would be able to resist him if he chose to exert the full force of his charm?

The only way she could count on being safe was to get away from here as quickly as possible.

As though she'd been tuning in to Jenna's thoughts, Suzie said wistfully, 'I wish we could stay here forever. Don't you?'

Jenna bit her lip to keep from giving the answer she'd really like to give.

'It's nice here,' she said, stooping to hold Suzie within the circle of her arms, 'but I think you'll like it even more at Aunt Louise's riding school. There will be lots of horses there to choose from, and, if you like, you can have proper lessons, beginning tomorrow, when we leave here.' She crossed her fingers, hoping she wasn't promising the impossible.

Suzie's face fell. 'But I don't want to leave. Duncan said I could stay as long as I wanted.'

Jenna's lips tightened, but she softened them into a smile. It was pointless to spoil Suzie's innocent enjoyment by showing her antagonism towards their host.

'That's kind of Duncan,' she said with reasonable calm, 'but we came here to help Aunt Louise. She needs us at the riding school. You don't want to let her down, do you?'

Suzie's mulish expression warned of an impending storm and Jenna bit her lip. Perhaps it was better to leave the argument for now, rather than let it become an issue. If Duncan kept his word, they would be leaving tomorrow, and she would just have to cross the bridge of Suzie's opposition when she came to it.

But, just to be sure, perhaps it was time she thought of making her own arrangements.

'Don't think about it now, pet. Just enjoy yourself and I'll see you later.'

Back at the house, she spent some time debating with herself on the best course of action, before she rang the riding school. The ringing tone went on for a while and Jenna was on the point of giving up when a male voice spoke.

'Stuart Anderson.'

'Oh, Stuart!' Jenna started a little. She'd heard the name a lot over the past days but it was something of a shock to be speaking to her cousin at last. 'I was expecting Aunt Louise to answer. It's Jenna.'

A rich laugh echoed down the line.

'Well, Cousin Jenna. How are you? I've just heard about your mishap from Mother. As luck had it, I've been away for a couple of days. Otherwise, I'd have been over there to pick you up before this.' Then, with an edge to his voice. 'We can't go on putting Fergusson to an inconvenience indefinitely, can we?'

Jenna felt decidedly uncomfortable. Until now, she'd felt the brunt of only one side of the feud. Now, from her cousin's tone, she realised that he felt every bit as much antagonism as Duncan Fergusson, and she had no wish to fan the flames of hatred on either side. Perhaps it might have been better, after all, to have waited to see whether Duncan's promise was fulfilled, before making this call. But it was too late now.

'No. That's why I'm ringing. Suzie and I'll be at Glenrae tomorrow, so tell Aunt Louise not to worry. Mr Fergusson has said he'll bring us over.'

'Good of him.' Stuart said disparagingly. 'But he needn't bother. I'll fetch you myself. Now, if you like.'

'Oh, no! Please!' Jenna broke in quickly. 'It's all been arranged. I don't know what time, but I'll see you and Aunt Louise tomorrow.'

There was a moment's hesitation, before Stuart gave a short laugh.

'Until tomorrow, then. I'll be waiting.'

Jenna's heart was thudding uncomfortably as she put the telephone down. The last thing in the world she wanted was a confrontation between the two men.

With a bit of luck, Duncan would keep his promise, and there would be no need for him to know she had even spoken to her cousin.

Jenna was happy to see that Suzie's expression was sunny again when she joined her for tea. Her day in the fresh air had certainly put the roses back into her cheeks and made her blue eyes shine. It looked as though the effects of the accident were beginning to disappear, Jenna thought with relief.

Jenna was feeling more like herself too. The warm sunshine had raised her spirits. And, now she knew she would be leaving the next day, one way or the other, for definite, she found she was almost looking forward to having dinner with Duncan Fergusson.

She dressed carefully in a dress of soft powder-blue, which enhanced the violet of her eyes. The plunge of the neckline was deep enough to be tantalising, but not so deep as to be openly revealing. A small devil whispered in her ear. Why not play him at his own game? Her heart skipped a beat. It would be a dangerous game, but how ironic if it was he who fell in love.

CHAPTER FIVE

AT THE door of the dining-room, Duncan paused to
let Jenna go in ahead of him. She glanced up warily.

'Don't worry.' He smiled mockingly. 'I'm not going
to eat you. Even up here in the Highlands, we're really
quite civilised. We hardly ever have guests on the
menu.'

'You surprise me,' Jenna bit back.

He laughed and drew out a chair for her to sit,
before moving around to seat himself opposite at the
long polished table.

He rang a bell and Annie came with the soup, her
observant eyes darting from one to the other as they
sat in silence, an oddly disapproving frown on her
face as she withdrew.

Duncan's gaze rested disconcertingly on Jenna as
she took up her spoon to eat. She did it carefully, so
that he wouldn't see how much her hands were trembling. No one had ever made her so nervous.

Then he began eating at last, releasing her from his
close attention, so that she was able to enjoy the
fragrant soup and fresh home-baked roll.

'Well,' he said, as he pushed back his empty bowl,
'did you enjoy your day.'

'Yes,' she answered distantly. 'I went down to the
stables. Suzie was there . . . helping out.'

'Yes. I know. I took her down there myself.'

'So I heard.' Jenna frowned, remembering her suspicions. 'And, since it was you who insisted she needed rest, I wonder why you did.'

He gave her an answering frown. 'Would you prefer it if she hung about the house all day feeling bored?'

Jenna bit her lip. 'No, of course not. But I don't want her to get...' She stopped, feeling flustered. She'd been about to say 'too attached to you', but that would have sounded foolish. 'She doesn't belong here and I don't want her to begin feeling that she does. There isn't any point.'

'Does there have to be a point to *everything*?' he asked, the last word stressed and edged with irritation.

'There usually is,' she said. 'However well disguised.'

He frowned. 'An intriguing statement. Would you care to explain it?'

'Not particularly. I think I'll leave it to your imagination.'

Jenna's heart fluttered uncomfortably. She had brought the battle to him, instead of waiting for the anticipated cat-and-mouse game, but she was already half regretting it as he caught her in the glare of cold eyes.

'Imagination seems to be more your forte. I wonder what it's cooking up now?'

Ignoring the goad, Jenna said tensely, 'We're leaving tomorrow, so there isn't any point in anything. To be honest, I'm getting rather tired of this stupid battle of wits we seem to be endlessly fighting.'

'Then why don't we stop?' He put his hand on her arm, where the warm strength of his fingers penetrated the thin material of her sleeve, quickening her pulse.

His smile was almost rueful. 'Somehow you seem to bring out the worst in me.'

Jenna eyed him defensively, the threatening tears drying in the heat of her indignation as she demanded, 'Are you blaming me for that?'

To her surprise, he laughed, sounding genuinely amused. 'I ought to. You have a habit of taking everything I say and twisting it into an argument.'

She regarded him with a frown, before admitting, 'Maybe that's because I don't trust you.'

He nodded. 'Perhaps I've been having the same trouble.'

Jenna caught her breath in soundless surprise at the sudden warm glow that lighted his eyes.

He squeezed her arm gently. 'What do you say we call a truce and just enjoy one another's company?'

Jenna found herself wavering. Was it possible he was really trying to bury the hatchet? Yes, probably in my skull, she thought with an attempt at wry humour.

He was quietly waiting for her answer.

What was there to lose? she asked herself. It was only for one more night.

'All right,' she said at last. 'Why not?'

He nodded. 'So, now for the next course.' He rang the brass bell with a flourish, designed to amuse her.

She gave him a cool smile. Mistrust died hard.

But, as the meal went on, Jenna found herself gradually unwinding. He really could be quite charming when he tried, and it was an effort to maintain her wariness. She found herself studying him in odd moments when he was engrossed. It was useless to deny that she was drawn to him, like a vulnerable moth to a bright flame, and she knew she could perish just as easily.

His eyes turned suddenly in her direction, meeting her gaze as it lingered on his face.

Jenna gave a guilty start and looked quickly away, but not before she saw a strange, smouldering question burning there. Her thoughts, at that moment, had little to do with guarding herself against him.

He was a man of magnetism and when he projected that magic towards her, as he was doing now, she found it hard to resist.

His eyes gleamed brightly at her and his mouth curved in a sensuous movement that became a smile.

Fascinated, she remembered that they were the same lips that had crushed hers in passionate punishment only hours before, forcing her almost to the brink of some great discovery, before suddenly rejecting her. She tried to revive her anger at the memory, but it melted with distressing rapidity as he took her hand in his. She could feel a pulse beating madly at the base of her throat and swallowed, her eyes fixed on his face.

He reached across and touched her cheek. Unnerved by his gentleness, Jenna sat still, her insides seeming to melt as his fingers began an exploration of the contours of her face, lingering on the curve of her lips. Strange longings stirred unknown depths ... painful yearnings ... for ... she knew not what.

'You look very lovely tonight,' he said softly. 'And that dress is very becoming.'

'Thank you. I'm glad you like it.' She looked down at the dress and suffered a jolt. How could she have forgotten? 'It was a gift from a friend.'

Martin had given it to her for a birthday present. The gift had meant so much to her, but now, incredibly, it seemed it was just a dress. She'd put it on without even remembering.

'A male friend, of course?' His voice broke into her reverie, sounding too casual.

'Yes.' Jenna was still a little bemused.

'Ahh! A close male friend, I take it.' He sounded almost annoyed, she noted in surprise.

She answered him shortly, 'Yes. But if you don't mind I'd rather not discuss it.'

He smiled. 'Is it painful.'

'Not particularly. Just private.'

'Forgive me.' He gave a short laugh. 'But I haven't noticed you being very observant of privacy.'

Jenna's face flamed. 'That wasn't very friendly. I thought we'd called a truce.'

'I thought so too. And I'm just trying to show a little friendly interest.'

'It seems more like the third degree to me,' she flared. 'But if you're really that interested,' she put down her knife and fork and looked straight at him, 'Martin and I were going to be married, until my parents died in a boating accident. When he realised he would have to take responsibility for Suzie also, he called off the wedding.' She gave him a pained smile. 'Not that interesting a story really, is it?'

'It's an idiotic story. The man's a fool.'

'Perhaps.' Jenna took a deep breath and let it out slowly and it seemed as though she was breathing out the last remnants of past pain.

She returned her attention to her food, but felt the force of his gaze still on her and looked up again.

'The accident to your parents,' he said, 'how did it happen?'

She gave a small bitter sigh.

'No one can say for sure. Dad was a keen fisherman and my mother enjoyed boating, so they often went out together in their small dinghy. One day there was a sudden fierce squall at sea ... and ...'

He took her hand, his fingers lightly caressing her palm in a strangely intimate gesture, spreading wildfire through her veins.

'So now there's just you and Suzie.'

'Yes. Just the two of us.' She shrugged. 'Life goes on and we make the best of it.'

He regarded her intently, with eyes that had definitely softened, making her feel distinctly uncomfortable.

She pulled her hand from his, meeting his gaze with sudden hostility. Why had she allowed herself to confide in him? The more he knew about her, the more power it would probably give him.

'So you came to Glenrae to mend a broken heart?' The question was soft and she thought she detected a hint of mockery.

Jenna glared at him. 'It wasn't like that.'

He lifted his dark brows. 'Then what was it like?'

'Aunt Louise invited me up for the summer and I accepted.'

He nodded. 'And when your aunt issued her invitation, she made no mention of her ... darling son?'

Jenna's eyes flickered. 'She mentioned him, of course. She could hardly avoid it, since it's his riding school we're being asked to help at.'

He snorted cynically. 'They need help as much as they need a hole in the head. And even if they did, there are plenty of horse-mad youngsters in the village who would be only too willing to lend a hand for next to nothing.'

'Then why should my aunt ask me to come?'

'An interesting question.' He raised his dark brows. 'To use your own words, there's usually a point to everything, however well disguised.'

Anger tightened into a knot inside her. To think that, for a little while, he had lulled her into thinking they could have a reasonable conversation.

'Are we talking about Marianne's ridiculous insinuations now?'

'Are they ridiculous?'

'Absolutely,' she bit back. 'There is no way my aunt would be trying to get Stuart and me together deliberately.'

'Why not? You're related to her by blood, but not to him,' he asserted coolly. 'It could be the ideal solution from her point of view. She's probably fool enough to believe marriage would calm her wild stepson into settling down. And it would solve the problem of yourself and Suzie being alone down south.'

Jenna's eyes rounded in mock amazement. 'The perfect scheme, of course,' she said sarcastically. 'Actually, now you've put it into words, it seems like a very good idea. And if Stuart is as handsome as his photograph, and he does propose, I think I'd be a fool not to consider it very seriously.'

'Oh, some women fall for Anderson, all right.' He made a derisive sound. 'But somehow I didn't think you were the type to go for looks or convenience.'

Jenna smiled sweetly. 'Didn't you? Well, actually, both would be of prime consideration.'

His eyes narrowed on her. 'I really must remember that.'

'Do!'

She stood up. 'I don't think I'll stay for coffee. Please tell Annie the meal was delicious. I'll thank her myself in the morning.' She gave him a sarcastic smile. 'In the meantime, thanks for a lovely evening.'

'It has been fascinating, hasn't it?' His voice was cool, his face unreadable.

'But not particularly entertaining,' she bit back.

He gave a short laugh. 'My apologies. I'll try harder next time.'

'I'm sure you would...if there was a next time,' she said coldly. 'But, happily, I'm leaving tomorrow. Don't say you've forgotten.'

'How could I, when you take every opportunity to remind me?'

'Yes.' There was no arguing with that. 'Well, then, I'll say goodnight.'

Much to her surprise, he didn't argue, but simply nodded and stood also, walking to the long windows to stare out at the night sky. He replied abstractedly to her stiff, 'Goodnight,' seeming not to notice as she left the room.

She called in on Suzie on the way up. The bedside light was still on and Edward Bear had fallen out of bed. With a smile, Jenna bent to retrieve him. He was beginning to look the worse for wear, with one eye missing and various parts of his anatomy practically threadbare. Poor old thing, she thought affectionately, he'd stood up to some hard times too.

She tucked him back into bed beside Suzie, whose cheeks were rosy with sleep. She touched her fingers against the warm skin. Was it imagination or was

Suzie a little feverish? But the little girl was sleeping peacefully enough. Turning out the light, Jenna crept softly away to her own room.

But, tired though she was, she found it hard to sleep. The events of the evening kept intruding into her mind. There had been times when she'd thought she was beginning to know Duncan Fergusson a little, but the moments had been brief and fraught with doubt.

He was hard, sophisticated, sure of his power over women, and unafraid of using that power if it suited his purpose. Even now, with his hatred for her relatives all too obvious, she could still fall easy prey.

Tonight, he had shown some kindness, some concern, and she had felt herself warming to him. But then his bitterness against Stuart Anderson had crept in once more between them, reminding her that what he allowed her to see was only the tip of an unfathomable iceberg.

She groaned, turning her face into her pillow, thanking some provident heaven for the fact that tomorrow she would be leaving this house.

Incredibly, she felt a sudden emptiness at the thought and shook herself mentally. This was no time to weaken. If she could just hang on to her own hatred, she would have a strong weapon against him.

CHAPTER SIX

A SHRILL noise filled the air and it was some time before Jenna could translate it into the frightened wail of a child.

Suzie! She shot out of bed, stumbling over her slippers in her haste to get to the door, but as she propelled herself out into the corridor the loud shrieks had already begun to subside.

Suzie was out in the corridor and a man's tall figure was stooping, holding the little girl reassuringly.

Jenna, who had begun to run, was brought up short by the sight of Duncan lifting her sister up in his arms. The child clung tightly around his neck, her small head buried against his shoulder. As Jenna moved forward more slowly, he lifted a finger to his lips, urging her to silence.

'She's not really awake,' he whispered. 'And she's calmer now.'

'What happened?' she mouthed to him, and he gave a slight shrug, his eyes indicating Suzie's bedroom door. He moved carefully towards it and Jenna followed, trembling with reaction, as he laid the sighing child gently in her bed. She watched in amazement as he tenderly covered her sister's small body and smoothed her damp forehead with a light hand.

Suzie murmured drowsily, 'I had a dream.'

'I know, my sweet. But you're all right now.'

The blue eyes began to flutter open. 'Where's Jenna?'

'I'm here, pet.' Jenna took her hand and squeezed it reassuringly. 'Go back to sleep.'

Suzie sighed and closed her eyes.

They stood together, in silence, waiting until the child had settled and then quietly left.

Outside in the corridor, Jenna let out her breath.

'She hasn't had one of those dreams for ages. I thought she'd got over them.'

'Come downstairs,' he commanded quietly, 'and I'll get you a brandy.' He took her hand quite naturally to lead her down the staircase. 'I could do wi' a wee dram m'sel'. I'd forgotten how harrowing a child's nightmares could be.'

She noted the unconscious broadening of his accent, a result, she guessed, of stress, and found it strangely endearing.

In the living-room, Duncan went straight to the drinks cabinet and took out two glasses and a bottle.

'Drink this.' He handed her a glass with a generous amount of spirit. 'It'll do you good. You look as shaken as I feel.' He took a long swallow of his own drink. 'My God! I needed that!'

Jenna sipped at her drink, grateful for its quicksilver warmth, and looked up at him almost shyly.

'It was very kind ... what you did for Suzie.'

'Natural reaction,' he said with a shrug.

But not for all men, Jenna thought. He really was a Jekyll and Hyde character. Which was the real Duncan Fergusson? she wondered, knowing it would be dangerous to try and find out.

She'd swung from one shade of opinion to another all evening and had had no relief from her thoughts of him even when she'd reached the sanctuary of her room. And now fate, in the shape of Suzie, had got her out of her bed for a second helping of whatever he intended to dish out.

He finished his drink in one swallow and rubbed his long fingers against the sides of his temples, as Jenna watched him in silence.

After a while, he stood up and crossed to the window. 'It's a lovely night out. Why don't we take a stroll . . . blow away the cobwebs?'

Jenna wondered what cobwebs he meant. Cobwebs of the past . . . or was that too much to hope for?

He crossed quickly and took her hand in his, pulling her to her feet. Jenna felt the familiar surge of excitement at his touch and allowed herself to be drawn out on to the terrace.

'Are you cold?'

Jenna shook her head, her defences breached a little by his thoughtfulness, and she made no protest as he slipped his arm about her waist to lead her down a curving pathway. She felt an urge to slip her own arm about his waist, draw closer to him. No doubt the brandy, which she'd drunk too fast, was to blame for the odd volatility of her emotions, and she warned herself to take care as heat from his body burned through her, setting her pulses racing madly.

The night air was warm, flower-scented, the sky dark and hung with tiny diamonds. The pale crescent of the moon barely touched with silver the wide lawn and shrubbery beyond. It was a scene of enchantment that sent a shiver of appreciation through Jenna's slender frame.

'You are cold.' He drew her more closely against him.

'No.' Jenna's voice was low and husky. 'Just overcome by the beauty of this place. It's so lovely.'

He turned her to him and scanned her face. 'Will
you be sorry to leave here?'

Caught off guard, Jenna answered him truthfully.
'In a way, yes, I will.' Then, seeing the gleam of
something indefinable in his dark eyes, she rushed on.
'But I suppose the countryside won't be too different
in Glenrae.'

She felt him stiffen. 'Is it only the countryside we're
discussing?'

He looked at her with eyes that were suddenly dark
and Jenna felt a tremor of excitement, intermingled
with fear.

'It's what I was discussing,' she answered carefully.

He smiled a little cynically. 'I didn't realise you were
such a nature-lover.'

'There's a lot you don't know about me.'

He heaved a sigh. 'That's true. It's a situation that
could be remedied if you'd let down your guard once
in a while.'

She laughed shortly. 'That's rich, coming from you.
Considering I know even less about you.'

'Really?' He raised one brow mockingly. 'Then why
do I get the impression you find me painfully
transparent?'

'Your motives, perhaps,' she agreed. 'And if we're
going to quarrel again, I'd rather go indoors and get
some sleep.'

He grasped her arm and she saw his mood had
changed.

'That's the last thing I want, Jenna . . . to quarrel
with you.'

'Then what . . . ?' she asked irritably.

With a growl of frustration, he gathered her suddenly into his embrace. Crushed against his chest, she

could feel the strong, pulsating rhythm of his heart against her own, and they seemed to beat as one.

He bent his dark head, and the fierce touch of his lips ignited her senses immediately. A swooning weakness seemed to take hold of her and her mouth yielded willingly to his. A shiver of ecstasy rippled through her as his hands began to roam possessively, pushing aside the low neckline of her nightdress. He gave a deep sigh and his mouth left hers to trace a path along her throat and on down to her exposed breast.

Freed from his lips, Jenna gasped in the cool air, bringing her to stinging awareness of what was happening. As his mouth touched her sensitised skin, she gasped and began to writhe in protest, her hand dragging at his hair to pull up his head.

For a moment, he mistook her movements for an increase in passion and responded exultantly, crushing her against him, increasing the demands of his mouth, but as her struggles became almost frantic he lifted his head at last and looked up into her face.

'What is it?' he asked raggedly.

'Stop it!' she cried, her breathing as torn and rasping as his own. Shamed by the force of her own emotions, by the strength of desire he'd aroused in her.

'Do you mean you weren't enjoying what was happening?' He gave a thin smile. 'That's not how it came across to me.'

She met his gaze angrily, a confusion of thoughts racing through her head. He seemed capable of wanting her and hating her almost at one and the same time.

'There's no depths to which you won't sink in order to get what you want, are there?'

He snorted. 'It seemed for a while we both wanted the same thing. Was I wrong?'

'Not entirely.' It was impossible to deny her response to him. They had both felt it. 'I admit you turned me on there for a moment. It won't happen again.'

His mouth curled at the corners. 'Don't give any written guarantees.'

His eyes glowed faintly in the moonlight and she returned his gaze, held by the flash of recognition that passed between them. The shock of it made her gasp.

He smiled and Jenna felt close to the edge of panic. Was that tenderness or triumph? Frightened, she began to pull away from him.

'I'm leaving tomorrow,' she said shakily, and it sounded like a prayer.

'You don't have to leave,' he said, his voice low and husky. 'You could stay here. Marry me.'

Jenna's heart came to a lurching stop and then regained momentum, thundering against her ribs so hard it was painful.

'You're asking me to marry you?'

He gave a brief, mirthless laugh. 'You're a beautiful, desirable woman. Is that so strange?'

She stared at him for a long moment, wishing she could see deep down into his shadowed soul. 'Very strange,' she said at last. 'Considering who I am.'

There was a deep, unnerving silence, during which they stared at one another, each wrapped in an individual anger.

He grasped her shoulders and shook her a little.

'You hard-headed, stubborn little fool,' he growled fiercely. 'Don't you ever give anyone the benefit of the doubt?'

Jenna glared defiantly. 'Not when there's too much doubt.'

'I've asked you to marry me,' he said doggedly, his fingers biting ruthlessly into her shoulders. 'I haven't yet had an answer.'

Jenna felt sick, drained, tired. How she wished that his proposal had been genuine, but it was a forlorn wish.

'My answer is no.' She met his probing stare unflinchingly, bright spots of colour burning in her otherwise pale face.

A taunting smile curved his lips. 'Would your answer be the same if it was Stuart Anderson who was doing the asking?'

Jenna exploded with rage, her violet eyes blazing. 'I don't know. I'll let you know if and when he asks me.'

He stared at her for long seconds and then he said, with apparent seriousness, 'I'm the better option.'

'That's just your opinion,' she jeered.

A taunting smile spread across his rugged face. 'Going on your reaction of a few moments ago, it seems it might be your opinion too.'

Jenna gasped. 'You don't miss a trick, do you?'

'Not too many, no.'

As she lifted her hand to strike him, he caught it, holding it with ease in his large palm.

'Don't fight me—marry me, sweet wild Jenna,' he said urgently. 'You admit you like it here, and you know there would always be a secure home for Suzie.'

Jenna was speechless with fury. How much lower was he going to sink? Bringing Suzie into it ... as though he cared a damn about her future.

'That's very altruistic of you,' she sneered. 'OK. So that's what would be in it for me. But what do you get out of it?'

He was silent for a moment, then he said quietly. 'I know what I hope to get out of it.'

She laughed sharply. 'Revenge, perhaps. For whatever you believe my cousin did to you.' She drew a sharp breath. 'Are you prepared to marry me just to make sure Stuart Anderson doesn't? Could you be miserable with a woman all your life, just to make sure he doesn't find happiness?'

He stared at her for long moments, his dark eyes pools of arid speculation. 'So you do intend to marry him?'

'Possibly. He might be just the kind of man I'm looking for,' she goaded. 'But I haven't even met him yet.'

He growled, a low hard sound. 'And you never would, if I had my way.'

'So now we've come to the truth, at last.' She stared at him. 'That's what this is all about, isn't it? Your proposal is just a stupid last-ditch attempt to keep me here ... away from him ...'

For a moment, he seemed almost as stunned as she, but she gave him no time to recover.

'Well, it didn't succeed. With your help, or without, Suzie and I will be going on to Glenrae tomorrow.'

Back in her room, Jenna was sitting at the open window in the faint light of dawn. Despite her physical exhaustion, her mind still ran riot. The ups and downs of the day had left her drained and uncertain, but an underlying current of excitement fluctuated with her thoughts.

Duncan had asked her to marry him. He couldn't be serious! He hardly knew her. No! It was all part of his campaign of torture, a knife-twist of vengeance. Mercifully, he couldn't know how much it hurt.

How he must be laughing at her, recalling the ease with which he could arouse her to passion. She despised herself for her weakness and it was hardly surprising that he despised her too. He'd taunted her with marriage, safe in the knowledge that she wouldn't dare accept him.

But what if she did dare? A small, insistent voice warned her that she was thinking dangerously, but the train of thought went on. What if she called his bluff? Would he really be prepared to go through a sham of a marriage to a stranger, simply to keep her from marrying Stuart Anderson?

She went cold deep inside at the thought of it. Proud he might be! Arrogant! Cruel! But was he cowardly enough to take out his spite on an innocent woman who had had the misfortune to cross his path?

She groaned, shaking her head from side to side. She would be willing to swear he was no coward. She was sure she had seen moments of real tenderness in him.

Vividly, in her mind, she saw him holding Suzie in his arms. The weeping child had been comforted, reassured . . . had allowed him to hold her. Didn't they say children instinctively knew when people were to be trusted?

Perhaps...a faint, hopeful voice whispered. Perhaps...if she were to marry him, she could show him that love was preferable to hate...that it was possible to forgive and forget...

As she mused, dawn gave way to the stronger light of early morning. Somewhere, outside in the yard, a door slammed.

She stood up, wincing as stiff muscles protested. How had she been so foolish as to spend the night in the armchair, instead of her nice comfortable bed?

The sound of a familiar male voice set her heart pounding and she peered furtively out of the window.

He was wearing his turned-down boots and the disreputable jacket she had first seen him in. So much had happened since then that it was impossible to believe that it was such a short while ago.

She leaned further out, wanting to see his face...wanting him to look up at her. Perhaps, in that first fresh glance, she might be able to gauge his real feelings for her.

But he was engrossed in attaching a horse box to the back of the Land Rover, his powerful arms manoeuvring the heavy shaft into position. A shudder ran through her. Those arms had held her last night, forcefully and yet gently, bending her to his will.

Alex, the carrot-haired boy from the stables, came from behind the vehicle to give a hand, but was waved away.

'It's done.' Duncan barked impatiently. 'You go and remind the lady that it's getting late.'

Jenna frowned, wondering which lady he meant. Was it herself? Was he going to take her on to Glenrae at last? But then, why the horsebox?

But she barely had time to wonder before she saw Marianne running lightly across the yard.

Duncan straightened as she drew near and Marianne flung her arms about his neck. He removed them irritably. 'Time and place, Marianne.'

'You are an old grouch lately.'

She tilted her head at Duncan, studying his solemn face with a tiny frown on her brow.

'I hope you're not going to be in one of your foul tempers all day. Because that would spoil all my plans.'

'I have plans of my own, Marianne,' he snapped. 'And they won't take up the whole day.'

He turned away and headed towards the house.

Jenna moved swiftly back from the window as Marianne's eyes turned upwards.

Minutes later, a knock sounded on her door. Duncan entered abruptly.

'Look, Jenna,' he began, 'I'm afraid there's something I must do this morning. Something important I'd forgotten. If you're still set on going to Glenrae, I will be back later to take you.'

'Oh, don't worry,' she answered stonily. 'I'm sure Marianne's plans are more pressing than mine.'

'Don't be petty, Jenna. It doesn't suit you. I've said I'll be back.'

She coloured hotly. 'So you did. But please don't rush. I've already made alternative arrangements. I telephoned my cousin yesterday and he'd be only too delighted to come and pick me up.'

'You did what?' He advanced towards her and Jenna almost retreated from the look of fury in his face. 'You invited Anderson here without my permission?'

She stood her ground. 'Do I need your permission to meet my cousin on the public highway? I didn't know you owned the world.'

'I don't intend to indulge in childish banter.' He gripped her arm fiercely. 'I've said I'll take you, and I will.'

'When you've finished indulging Marianne's whims?' Jenna's lip curled.

'Marianne has nothing to do with it.'

'Doesn't she?' Jenna felt the press of childish tears of disappointment, but didn't give way. 'You gave me your promise.'

'And I'll keep it,' he gritted, looking down into her angry face with an expression of steel. 'Just make sure you're ready and waiting when I get back.'

Jenna shook off his hand. 'Go to hell, Duncan Fergusson.'

He grinned unpleasantly. 'I dare say I will. But before I do, I'll take you to Glenrae and your precious family.'

Before she could gather breath for a retort, he'd turned and left, the door slamming hard behind him.

'I wouldn't bank on that,' she shouted after him, knowing the thick oak door withheld the sound. 'Damn the man,' she cursed ineffectually. Just who did he think he was? Lord and master of this house, perhaps, but not of her.

She bit her lip so hard that she almost drew blood. Did he imagine, she wondered mutinously, that she would spend the day waiting meekly for his return? Well, if he did, he would be in for a surprise. She would go to Glenrae today, if she and Suzie had to walk every step of the way.

But, hopefully, that wouldn't be necessary. A telephone call to her cousin Stuart would be all that was needed to relieve Duncan Fergusson of his unwelcome charges.

Duncan stood in the jamb of the huge barnlike doors, leaning his broad back against the weathered wood. The sun was warm and, at any other time, he might have enjoyed the colourful bustle that was going on around him.

But today he was conscious of tension, like a coiled spring, drawing tighter as time ticked inexorably by. For the tenth time in an hour, he glanced at his watch, smiling satirically to see that it was only three minutes later than the last time he had looked.

Where was Hugh, dammit? He was supposed to be bringing the colt today, and he was damned if he was going to leave without it now.

He straightened up as he saw Marianne walking a spirited roan and wearing her catlike smile, her green eyes sparkling with satisfaction. She'd get what she wanted. Didn't she always? he commented wryly to himself, as he watched her bewitching Edward Buchanan out of his prized hunter for a good deal less than he was realistically worth.

'Won't be long,' she called. 'There's just the paperwork.'

He grimaced and looked at his watch again, noting, with a snort of impatience, that it was getting close to noon. He had promised Jenna that he would be home in time to take her to Glenrae and, while he had no intention of doing so if he could possibly persuade her to stay, he'd have to get back soon.

Something descended heavily on to his shoulder, startling him back to the present, and a broad, weathered hand was thrust into his.

'Duncan, my boy!' Hugh Ingram's ruddy face beamed at him. 'Waiting for me?'

'Hugh! You old dog. You're late.'

Hugh's eyes twinkled. 'Ah. So, you're interested in some of my stock.'

Duncan hadn't time to haggle. 'Only one. The black yearling.'

Marianne returned five minutes later, surprised to find Duncan leading the black horse into the box beside her roan.

'Darling,' she exclaimed, 'have you bought me a present?'

Her eyes gleamed greedily at the sight of the well-proportioned thoroughbred.

'No,' Duncan replied shortly. 'I want him myself.'

He pulled up the ramp and locked it. 'Are you ready to leave?'

Marianne frowned. 'Why are you in such a hurry? You've been like a caged lion all morning.'

'Sorry,' he said without conviction. 'But today wasn't particularly convenient. I've something to attend to at home.'

'Don't tell me what that business is. Let me guess.' Marianne bit her lip. 'Damn you, Duncan. Can't you spare just one day for me?'

'Sorry,' he said again, his gaze flicking impatiently over her petulant face, wondering why he had ever found Marianne's tricks amusing. 'Some other day perhaps.'

Her mouth twisted. 'Don't do me any favours.'

He moved around to the front of the Land Rover and opened the passenger door.

'Are you going home, or do you want me to drop you off somewhere?'

With a look that pierced him through, she stalked past him in haughty silence and climbed into the front seat, her jaw clamped in white fury.

They accomplished the journey to Marianne's large, luxurious house in silence. He drove around the side to the stables and pulled up. She got out before he could get around to help her.

'I won't delay you,' she said coldly. 'Put Red in the yard and Alfred will take care of him.'

With no time to argue her peremptory command, he brought the hunter out of the box and handed him over to Marianne's stable lad and got back into his vehicle, filled with a sudden sense of urgency.

The distance between Marianne's house and his own seemed endless. Driven by a coiled expectancy, he found it hard to keep to a speed that was comfortable for the beast he carried in the back.

The house was in sight at last and he manoeuvred the vehicle and box into the turn-off that led to his front entrance. Trees hid the gates from his view, but, to one side, he thought he could see a vehicle parked in the road. He groaned with annoyance. An unexpected visitor to delay him still further? But who?

As he drew closer, he saw Jenna, with Suzie's hand in hers, coming out of the gates. Her face seemed pale, but she was wearing a smile for the man who stood waiting for her.

Suddenly, he was able to identify the vehicle and the man. It was Stuart Anderson. Black fury engulfed him as he drew to a halt and jumped out.

Jenna saw Duncan thundering towards them and blanched.

'I told you I'd be back,' he growled at her. 'I thought you might have had the courtesy to wait.'

'I couldn't take a chance.' Jenna said defiantly. 'Now it doesn't matter; Stuart is here to take us.'

Duncan turned his attention to the man who stood looking at him with a thin smile on his face.

'So I see,' he gritted. 'I must say, Anderson, I didn't think you'd have the gall to turn up here.'

'Then you're obviously not thinking straight.' Stuart Anderson hunched his shoulders aggressively. 'I had no hesitation in answering my sweet cousin's call for help.'

Duncan's dark scowl deepened. 'She was in no danger from me.'

'For heaven's sake.' Jenna cut in. 'We're not bones to be fought over by dogs. We just want to get to Glenrae.' She looked down at her sister, who looked pale and a little frightened. 'Can't you see this is upsetting Suzie?'

'It's a pity you didn't consider her feelings before doing what you did.' Duncan looked at the little girl and his mouth set grimly. 'But that's not the point right now.'

He bent to Suzie and ruffled her curls. 'Sorry you had to leave in a hurry, little one, but I dare say we'll bump into one another again soon.'

'Do you think so?' Suzie's face brightened.

Duncan pinched her cheek. 'I think so. In fact you can bank on it.'

Jenna bit her lip to keep from telling him he had no right to promise Suzie anything of the sort, but her sister was happy again and she had no wish to cause another upset by arguing.

She flashed a restraining glance at Stuart as he seemed about to issue a challenge. 'We'd better be going. Aunt Louise will be wondering what's keeping us so long.'

Duncan's eyes were on her, dark and cold, as she turned to him, unsure how she was going to effect her goodbyes.

She held out her hand and he shook it briefly, dropping it so swiftly that it might have been a burning brand.

'If you're thinking of thanking me,' he said, uncannily reading her mind, 'there's no need. It's been my pleasure.'

'I'll bet it has.' Stuart cut in grittily. 'And now it's mine.' He picked Suzie up in his arms. 'Let's go, shrimp.'

Jenna, her eyes drawn to Duncan Fergusson's face, saw a shadow pass over it, a look so bleak and hard that it made her shiver.

'To every dog its day,' he said in a low voice which nevertheless carried to them all. 'And soon it will be mine.'

CHAPTER SEVEN

STUART came breezing into the kitchen, where Jenna was helping her aunt to wash the breakfast dishes.

'I thought I'd find you here,' he said lightly, tugging teasingly at Jenna's hair. 'Before you get your nose too firmly to the grindstone, how about taking a stroll with me into the village? There are one or two things I need to pick up and then we can have a look around Glenrae together.'

He grinned at her and she was struck again by his unexpected looks. She'd thought he would be dark, with a rugged Scottish face, like Duncan, but he was blond, with almost delicate Nordic features making her wonder if some of his distant relatives had, in fact, been Scandinavian.

In the two weeks she'd been at the school, they'd established an easy friendship.

'I don't know if I can spare the time,' she said, looking at her aunt. 'We have an awful lot to do this morning.'

'Nonsense,' Louise broke in. 'There's nothing that can't wait. You go and have some fresh air. It will put some colour into your cheeks.' She patted Jenna's shoulder fondly. 'I can't understand why you're still so pale. Perhaps Stuart is right and we're working you too hard.'

Jenna looked away, glad her aunt couldn't see into her mind to explore the cause of her wan looks. She was reluctant to explore the reason herself. She wasn't sleeping well and woke each morning feeling tired and strangely empty.

During the day, when her time was filled with the task of dealing with the surprisingly large amount of correspondence, accounts and enquiries that were part of running the school, and helping her aunt about the house, she hardly had time to think.

But at night her thoughts turned inevitably to Duncan Fergusson. It was ridiculous to think she could be missing him, but she couldn't help wishing it had been possible to leave him on a more friendly footing. When he hadn't been allowing his hatred to come between them, he had been kind. But then, she reminded herself dolefully, even that had probably been part of his plan of campaign, along with his surprising proposal of marriage. It had been an obvious taunt, meant to humiliate her, and he probably hadn't even expected a proper answer.

'My mother thinks you should have some air,' Stuart cut into her reverie. 'And she always gets her own way, so you'd better give in.'

Jenna smiled at this unsubtle blackmail.

'That makes it two against one, so I suppose I'd better.'

She went upstairs to fetch a warm cardigan and a pair of comfortable shoes. Stuart was waiting in the hall when she came down again.

'I take it we're walking?'

Stuart nodded. 'If you think you can manage it. It's about two miles to the village—all downhill. And, if you don't feel up to the climb back up, we could always cadge a lift from someone.'

'I'll manage.' Jenna sighed. 'Now you mention it, I'm just longing for some real exercise.'

'Then let's go.'

It was a beautiful morning. The surrounding countryside was at its best, the rugged sweep of the valley softened by a faint mist which arose from a distant loch. To the right, an area of moorland stretched, desolate and splendid, with only a single cottage visible close to an old wood.

Stuart pointed into the distance. 'There are lots of little bays on the north shore of the loch. If you like wild birds, there are plenty to be seen along that stretch. We could take a trip there one day if you'd like.'

'That would be lovely.'

Why, Jenna wondered, did she suddenly see Duncan's face in her mind's eye? Would it always be only him she would associate with this wild and beautiful landscape?

As Stuart had said, the road wound downhill and walking took no effort. From this point, they looked down on a stone church, set on rising ground, and, not too far into the distance, Jenna could see a cluster of houses that heralded the start of the village.

They walked steadily on and it wasn't long before they were close to the lych-gate of the church. Jenna paused to look over the mossy wall. The bright sun shone on the weathered gravestones and flowers growing in the well-tended borders.

'Do you want to go in and take a closer look? Or do graveyards frighten you?'

'No. They don't,' Jenna denied. 'As a matter of fact, I rather like to browse through really old head-stones. They tell so much about the history of a place and the families who've lived there.'

'Well, this one will certainly tell you a lot about my family ancestors. Most of them are buried here.' He made a wry sound. 'One or two escaped to foreign lands, but not many of them.'

'That's an odd way of putting it—escape.' Jenna looked at him curiously as he opened the gate for her to pass through. 'Do you want to leave Glenrae?'

'Maybe...sometimes!' He shrugged. 'Mostly, I'm happy enough.'

'Then you're lucky.' Jenna said a little wistfully. 'Sometimes, being alone isn't all it's made out to be.'

'Oh, sure! The other man's grass works both ways.' Stuart gave a short laugh. 'And actually, I do know what it's like out there in the wide world. I left home for a while a couple of years back.'

Jenna stopped short as she saw Stuart's rather full lips drawn into a grim line.

'Didn't it work out? Were you homesick?'

'I don't really remember,' he said, and Jenna had the feeling he was being evasive. 'I just came back.'

She wandered away from him to a sunny corner and began reading the stones. She paused as she realised more than one of them bore the name Fergusson.

Stuart came and stood beside her as she looked down at a fairly recent stone which was inscribed to Shauna Fergusson and her child Marie.

Jenna's heart started to beat fast. 'Duncan Fergusson's wife and child?' she queried faintly. She hadn't even considered the idea that he might be a widower. She thought suddenly of the nursery she had invaded and felt the dawn of understanding.

'No,' Stuart said. 'His sister and little niece.' He hesitated before going on. 'They died in a road accident up on the ridge two years ago.'

There was a catch in his voice and Jenna spun round to see his face. It was dark and clouded.

'Was she a . . . friend . . . of yours?'

He made a short sound. 'Something like that.'

In a flash of insight, Jenna knew she'd found the reason for the feud between the two men.

'And . . . and Duncan thinks you're responsible for their deaths?'

Things were suddenly becoming very clear.

He said shortly. 'That's the way he tells it.'

Jenna prodded gently. 'And how do you tell it, Stuart?'

'I don't,' he said abruptly. 'I leave people to draw their own conclusions.' He made a short, unamused sound. 'They will anyway.'

Jenna shook her head doubtfully. 'If Duncan's got it wrong, you ought to tell him. He's very bitter against you.'

'I know. He hates me. But that's his problem.' Stuart shrugged and his mouth twisted. 'If he'd rather go on thinking the worst of his sister than know the truth . . .'

Jenna took his arm tentatively. 'I'd like to know the truth.'

'I'm sure you would,' he said, sounding cynical. He stopped suddenly to put his hands on her shoulders, looking down into her anxious face. 'And who knows? One day, I may tell you. But not just now.'

He gave himself a little shake and hooked an arm about her shoulders. 'Let's go on. We're supposed to be enjoying this walk.'

They halted in the little village square.

'I've got some business up in the saddlery that will take about an hour,' Stuart said. 'Do you want to come or would you prefer to do a little solitary exploring?'

'The second option, I think.'

Stuart nodded. 'OK. There's a bench over by the old schoolhouse,' he said. 'I'll meet you there in about an hour.'

He dropped a light kiss on her nose, before turning her in the right direction.

Jenna spent a pleasant hour looking around the village at the couple of shops which seemed, between them, to sell everything anyone could ever want, and the sturdy stone-built houses, which reminded her somehow of the people. Built to withstand the weather and life's other storms. As the dwellings became more scattered and the road began to lead out into the countryside again, she turned back to find the square.

She found the school and the bench Stuart had mentioned and sat down to wait for him. She was glad of the little rest, and leaned back with her eyes closed against the warmth of the sun. A light breeze fanned her cheeks and carried the tantalising scent of blossom. For a while, it was bliss.

But, inevitably, her thoughts turned to Duncan and what Stuart had told her in the churchyard, convinced that the story behind that was the cause of Duncan's behaviour. She couldn't help feeling some sympathy for him. He'd been right in one respect. Stuart's implication in the death of his sister and niece would hardly be a matter for petty spite. It might even justify his obviously strong animosity against her cousin, if it were true.

Stuart had implied Duncan had it wrong, and she'd been inclined to believe he'd been genuine, but it was hard to see how such a major lack in communication could have arisen between the two men. Did the hatred go even deeper?

But, whatever, she couldn't help feeling it gave no justification for Duncan's perverse behaviour towards herself.

'Well, hello, there, Miss Wilde!' The cool voice startled her into sharp awareness. 'You're wise to make the most of the warm spell. There's no telling when the next one will come along.'

Jenna opened her eyes with a start, to see Duncan Fergusson standing before her. Still deep in her thoughts of him, in a dazed moment she half believed she'd conjured him up.

His tall figure seemed to loom over her, blocking out the light and throwing the strong planes of his face into stark relief. He seemed even more handsome than she'd remembered and Jenna felt the uneven bumping of her heart in some annoyance.

'Thanks,' she said, with a calm she was far from feeling. 'I'll bear that in mind. I wouldn't want to miss anything.'

He sat down beside her, keeping a sedate distance between them. Jenna gritted her teeth. He was obviously still playing games.

'How are you settling in at the school?'

She studied his cool face deliberately. 'If you're really interested . . . I'm enjoying every minute.'

He nodded, unperturbed by this frosty reception. 'Glad to hear it. And young Suzie?'

'Never a dull moment.'

'Good.' He said pleasantly. 'By the way, you might tell her I have something special to show her, the next time she's up at the house.'

Jenna stared at him disbelievingly. 'Up at the house?' She echoed blankly. 'Do you mean your house?'

'Where else?' His dark brows arched faintly in amusement.

She said irritably, 'We're hardly likely to be at your house again, so I don't think there would be any point in relaying your message.'

'You're not coming to the fête at the weekend?' he queried lazily. 'It's the big event of the year. The good ladies of the locality like to hold their charitable event in my top field. I believe they serve a delicious high tea in the larger dining-room at the house.'

Which was a room Jenna hadn't seen, and probably never would now, she thought a little regretfully.

As though he'd read her mind, he said, 'You may remember I offered to show you around. If you're still interested, the fête would provide an ideal opportunity, with all those third parties around to make sure I didn't lock you up in some secret tower.' There was a gleam of ironic humour in his eyes.

'Thanks. But I think I'll be too busy to get away from the school.'

He made a soft mocking, tutting sound.

'It will be noted in the village if you don't come,' he insisted. 'Everybody does.'

Jenna smiled thinly. 'What? Everybody? Even the Andersons?'

Only the faintest flicker of an eyelid betrayed his feelings. He said evenly, 'They haven't put in an appearance of late, it's true.'

'Do you mean things have changed,' she persisted, 'and that this year my aunt and Stuart would be welcome to turn up?'

His firm mouth thinned. 'I think your cousin is a little more realistic than that,' he said bitingly.

'Ah! I see,' Jenna said coolly. 'Then, in that case, I don't think I'd be interested.'

'You seem interested enough in Anderson,' he growled. 'Do I take it your aunt's little scheme is progressing?'

Jenna frowned in puzzlement and then realised he must have seen Stuart's casual parting kiss.

'Take what you like,' she retorted. 'My relationship with my cousin is not your business.'

'I choose to think it is.' He moved closer, so that his face was no more than a breath away. 'We have some unfinished business, Jenna,' he said very softly.

She recoiled, shaken by the surge of excitement which ran through her at his nearness.

'I . . . I don't think so.'

He smiled coolly at her reaction. 'Is your memory that bad? I asked you a question. Don't you remember?'

'No,' she answered, just as cool. 'I don't remember your asking any *serious* question.'

'Oh, I was very serious.' His low voice had turned grim.

She raised her eyebrows derisively. 'You mean . . . your proposal of marriage?'

'That's what I mean. Stop playing coy, Jenna. It doesn't suit you.'

His eyes caught hers in a probing stare which made her angry.

'You seem to be an expert on what suits me.'

'I could be, given the opportunity.' He smiled. 'And what better opportunity than in marriage?'

The sexual implication was obvious and Jenna flushed.

She said tightly, 'I'm sure. But I've already given you my answer. No! However, thanks for the kind offer.'

'I wasn't being kind,' he gritted.

'I know.' Jenna confirmed fiercely. 'So what were you being?'

He gave a short, vexed laugh. 'I thought, by now, you might know.'

Jenna frowned, surprised by his reply and not sure what to make of it. 'Well, I don't.'

'I'm sure you would, if you thought about it.' He sighed heavily and stood up. 'So. I won't be seeing you at the fête?'

'No,' she answered uncompromisingly.

'That's a pity, for Suzie. Isn't it time you thought about giving her a little fun?'

Jenna gasped. 'My God! You don't pull any punches, do you?'

'Not when they're necessary. No.'

She breathed in sharply. 'Well, they're not necessary now. Practically everything I do is with Suzie's welfare in mind.'

'In that case, we might all meet again soon.' To her surprise, he leaned forward and placed a light kiss against her lips before walking away. '*Au revoir* for now,' he said sardonically.

Jenna slumped back into her seat, listening to her own ragged breathing and feeling a peculiar mixture of anger and elation.

Marianne was at the school when they got back. She shot a cool glance at Jenna and dragged Stuart into the office, shutting the door firmly behind them.

Jenna gave an exasperated sigh and went to busy herself in the storeroom.

She had been relieved to find that Marianne didn't live on the school premises and the times when she had come in during the past fortnight she'd seemed to keep deliberately out of Jenna's way.

The office adjoined the house, quite a distance from the stables and training paddocks, so it hadn't been a difficult thing to achieve.

The office door opened again some time later and Jenna heard Marianne's high, carrying voice.

'Now your little helper's arrived at last, I feel I'm entitled to take some leave. Lord knows I'm due it.'

'I don't mind you having the time off,' Stuart replied pithily. 'But I'd rather you didn't spend it in such bad company.'

'Meaning Duncan, of course.' Marianne grinned a little sourly. 'You and he are more two of a kind than you think.'

'Heaven forbid!' Stuart rapped cynically. 'The man's got a heart of ice. Just remember, if you hold on to it, ice burns.'

Marianne laughed. 'What makes you think I don't love that kind of heat?'

'Then take care. Ice-burns can leave scars.' Stuart said, adding drily, 'Let me know when you're up to coming back to work.'

Marianne smiled sweetly. 'Are you sure I wouldn't be playing gooseberry? You two seem to be getting along so well, I wouldn't want to spoil things for you.'

'I'm sure you would, if you could.' Stuart was unperturbed. 'But you won't.'

When she'd gone, Jenna tackled Stuart.

'Why did you say that?' she demanded in annoyance. 'About not letting her spoil things between us. You know what she was implying and I wish you'd put her straight rather than joking about it.'

'Marianne doesn't need things spelled out for her,' he said with a dismissive shrug. 'She enjoys her little games, but I shouldn't let it bother you.'

But it did bother her, she admitted worriedly.

Apart from the jealousy she stupidly felt at the thought that Duncan was spending his time with Marianne, she could do without Stuart stoking the flames of the girl's dislike. It was bad enough to have made one enemy already in her short stay, without deliberately adding another to the list.

CHAPTER EIGHT

DURING the days that followed, Jenna tried hard to put Duncan out of her mind. With a bit of luck, he had given up his ideas of revenge and, with a bit of extra luck, she might be able to relax and enjoy the remainder of her stay. But that, of course, was easier said than done.

She couldn't help wishing that it might be possible for them to be friends, but knew the idea was ridiculous. The tension that inevitably sparked between them would make that kind of association impossible. Far better to stay way from him. Out of sight, out of mind, as the old adage went. But then, why did the days feel so empty? And why should she still have such unwanted feelings for him?

In a way, she thought, it was almost inevitable that he should make a strong impact on her. He was so different from any other man she had ever met. Proud, forceful, tenacious and presently, it seemed, unforgettable. But perhaps, when she got back home, the memory of their meeting would take on the nature of a dream and fade as quickly.

The thought of going back home brought no pleasure. Duncan Fergusson apart, she was happy here—well suited to the varied life. And Suzie was thriving...looking far healthier and happier than Jenna had ever seen her.

She came in to tea with her cheeks rosy and her eyes glowing with excitement.

'There's a fête on at Duncan's house on Saturday,' she enthused. 'Are we going?'

Damn! Jenna muttered under her breath. She might have known Suzie would get to hear about it.

'I don't think so, pet. I'm going to be very busy on Saturday.'

Suzie's face crumpled. 'You're always busy these days. We never have any fun.'

Jenna bit her lip, stung by Suzie's words into remembering what Duncan Fergusson had said when they'd met in the village.

'Oh, Suzie!' She put her arm coaxingly about her sister's tense little shoulders. 'I thought you were having lots of fun here at the riding school.'

'Well, I am,' Suzie muttered grudgingly. 'But we never go out anywhere together, like we used to.'

Jenna was dismayed to realise that it was true. They hadn't once gone off together for the day as they invariably had on weekends at home. She could blame pressure of work at the school, but a lot of the time, she knew, she worked to keep her mind off Duncan.

'I'm sorry, Suzie,' she said contritely. 'I really am going to be busy on Saturday, but I'll make it up to you, I promise.'

Suzie turned her head away in silence, but not before Jenna saw the gleam of angry tears.

'How about Sunday?' she said hurriedly. 'Stuart offered to take us to the loch to look at the wild birds. We could go on Sunday.'

'If you're not going to be busy on Sunday,' Suzie turned a thoughtful look on her, 'why can't you work on Sunday and take me to the fête on Saturday.'

Jenna's mouth dropped. Pure logic at work to find a perfect solution. When had Suzie started to grow up?

Faced with such ingenuity, how could she possibly refuse? It might be possible, after all, to stay out of Duncan Fergusson's way.

'OK, clever boots. You win.'

'Oh, great!' Suzie gave Jenna a jubilant hug and went charging off down to the stables.

Saturday came, and, along with it, disaster.

'Oh, no!' Jenna sank down on to the wooden bench alongside the table in the kitchen. 'This would happen! Today of all days! My car won't start, and Stuart's taken the Land Rover for the day.'

'For goodness' sake, my dear, relax and I'll make you a nice cup of tea.' Louise plugged the kettle in and patted Jenna's shoulders. 'What's so important about today?'

Jenna took a deep breath. 'It's the day of the fête,' she said, a little more calmly. 'And I've promised Suzie I'd take her.'

'The fête.' Louise repeated, with a sigh. 'Ah, yes! Well it was always a good day out ... before——'

'Precisely.' Jenna cut in. 'Before ... but not any more ... not for the Andersons. Nor the Wildes either, I'm afraid.'

'So, you know that old story.' Louise gave her a vexed look.

'Some of it,' Jenna admitted. 'But I'd like to know the whole of it, then perhaps I might understand what's going on between Duncan Fergusson and Stuart.' Jenna paused. She'd thought before of asking Louise about the matter, but it had seemed like prying behind Stuart's back, but now the subject was broached.

'I don't know the whole of it myself,' Louise said soberly. 'Stuart refuses to comment, even to me. He says it was private, between him and Shauna.'

'Was he in love with her?' Jenna couldn't help the question.

'I honestly don't know. They seemed pretty friendly at the time, but Shauna was married and I think that would have mattered to Stuart. Whatever else he may be, I don't believe he's a home-breaker.'

'He might just as well have been,' Jenna said, 'as far as Duncan Fergusson is concerned.'

Louise tutted impatiently. 'Men, and their foolish pride!' She shook her head. 'An indispensable part of their make-up, I suppose. But, when it interferes with a child's innocent day out——'

'Speaking of which,' Jenna cut in hastily, 'what's happened to Suzie? She's really determined about that fête, and just wouldn't listen when I tried to explain to her about the car. Perhaps there's someone about who can get it going for me.'

'We'll see, after you've finished your tea,' Louise said comfortably. 'Calm down. The fête doesn't start until after lunch, so you've plenty of time yet.'

Jenna subsided with a sigh of relief. 'In that case, I'll have that cup of tea. I think I need it.'

But, as luck would have it, both stable lads had gone to the horse sale with Stuart. In desperation, Jenna telephoned the garage in the next village, but got no answer. Perhaps the mechanic was going to the fête as well, she thought wryly, and then sighed. It really looked as though she might have to disappoint Suzie after all.

She half thought of ringing Duncan to ask if he'd pick them up, but her pride balked at the idea of asking him for that favour, particularly as she'd haughtily told him she wasn't going. He would count her request as two victories.

She looked about for Suzie, but she was nowhere in evidence. Jenna guessed she was hiding away somewhere, sulking, and sighed wearily. She'd turn up eventually and then she would do her best to make Suzie understand that she'd tried, at least, to keep her promise.

An hour later, Suzie still hadn't put in an appearance. But it was only a matter of time, Jenna reasoned. Having refused her breakfast in temper, she was sure to be turning up shortly for her lunch. For a little one, her appetite for food was enormous, and everybody wondered where she put it all. Stuart laughingly accused her of having hollow legs.

But she didn't come up to the house for lunch, and it was then that Jenna really began to worry. A thorough search of the house, gardens and stables failed to uncover her hiding place.

Monica, the local girl who came in on Saturdays to help and who Suzie reported as being engaged to Duncan's stable lad, Alex, was there, grooming one of the horses.

'Have you seen Suzie?' Jenna asked, a little breathlessly.

Monica shook her head. 'Not recently. She was over there, with Cherry earlier.' She pointed to one of the stalls.

Jenna could see the stall was empty even from here, and her heart began to thud. 'Has Suzie gone riding alone?'

Monica frowned. 'I shouldn't think so. She's no-where near ready for that yet.'

'I know that,' Jenna said grimly. 'But does she?'

'I don't think she will have gone far.' Monica said reassuringly.

Jenna bit her lip. Surely Suzie wouldn't do a silly thing like that, not even in a temper? But the little minx was growing up fast, and developing a strong mind of her own.

She said to Monica. 'If you see her, will you tell her I'm looking for her and she's to come up to the house right away?'

'Yes, sure.' The girl said, with an indifferent shrug, turning back to her grooming.

Just as she was leaving the yard, Alex arrived, probably to pay Monica a visit, if Suzie was right.

Jenna hurried across to him. 'Alex, I can't find Suzie. You haven't seen her, I suppose?'

He grinned. 'I told her you wouldn't like it.'

Jenna's heart skipped a beat. 'Wouldn't like what?' she asked with grim suspicion.

'Her riding over to our place on her own,' Alex said blithely. 'But she wouldn't listen to me.' Seeing Jenna's horrified face, he went on quickly, 'She's safe enough on good old Cherry, and she's developed quite a good seat already, but I thought I'd better get over here and let somebody know what she's up to.'

'A good seat!' Jenna reiterated, feeling her temper rise. 'It'll be a very painful seat, by the time I've finished with that little madam.'

'In for a paddling, is she?' Alex's grin widened. 'You've got to admire her spirit, though. Haven't you?'

But Jenna was in no mood for admiration.

She cast an impatient eye about the stable. 'Can you throw a saddle on one of the horses for me, Alex,' she asked, 'while I just slip up to the house to change this skirt for breeches?'

'Sure. Would you like me to bring your mount on up to the house for you? Save you walking back down?'

'If you would. Thanks.'

The horse he brought her was young and faster than most of the others in the school, but, even so, she was in sight of Duncan's house without having seen any sign of her sister. Despite the delay in giving chase, it didn't seem possible old Cherry had made the journey in this good a time. Was it possible Suzie had had a fall somewhere along the way? Jenna wondered anxiously.

Gone were all thoughts of punishment. She would be thankful just to see Suzie all in one piece.

Duncan was in the stable yard when she arrived there.

'You're looking for young Suzie, of course,' he said, before she could speak.

Jenna let out her pent-up breath. 'Then she's here?'

He nodded. 'Arrived about fifteen minutes ago, asking to see the fête. It hasn't started yet, so I brought her down here.'

Fuelled by her anxiety, Jenna's temper flared. 'I don't suppose you thought to telephone.'

'I did.' He looked at her with one eyebrow raised satirically. 'I asked for you personally, but you weren't there. And now, of course, you're here.'

Jenna said stormily. 'Where's Suzie?' Now the crisis was over, she had an urge to wring her sister's neck.

'She's in the stable, admiring my new acquisition. Do you want to take a look too?'

He tried to take her arm, but she snatched it away.

'Have you any idea what I've been going through on the way over here?' she cried furiously. 'I've been imagining all sorts of terrible things...'

'I can well believe it,' he said calmly. 'But fortunately, none of them happened. Suzie's here, safe and sound.'

'With no discouragement from you, of course,' she accused hotly. 'No wonder she was so determined to come to your damned fête.'

His face hardened. 'Meaning?'

'Meaning...' Jenna's mouth stayed open. She wasn't quite sure what she meant, she only knew he was somehow to blame for this situation. She started again. 'Meaning I think somehow you engineered this.'

He gave a short unamused laugh. 'That's silly, Jenna. And you know it.'

He was frowning at her in exasperation, looking fantastic, despite the grim looks, in well-fitting fawn breeches and a dark tan polo neck. The sight of him had her insides fluttering like a hundred butterflies.

He waited calmly for her to respond, an enigmatic smile playing about his lips.

She fumed, 'You asked me to let Suzie know you had something "special" for her to see. Is that why she's here? Did you have your message delivered some other way? Alex visits the school pretty often, doesn't he?'

'I wouldn't know what Alex does on his time off.' He gave an exaggerated sigh. 'Look, Jenna! I know you don't exactly feel friendly towards me, but surely——'

'Friendly!' She cut in, on a note of incredulity. 'That's rich...considering that from the moment you found out I was related to the Andersons you've treated me like your deadliest enemy!' She was shaking from head to foot with temper. 'And all because of an accident that happened a long time ago. Something that you've allowed your mind to twist and distort out of all proportion——'

She drew sharply to a halt, appalled at having blurted that out.

He gasped and grabbed her arms, his eyes blazing with a fury that matched her own.

'My sister and her child died in that accident,' he hissed. 'An accident that would never have happened if Stuart Anderson hadn't led Shauna on.'

Jenna stared back into his blazing eyes. 'How can you be sure of that? Has it never entered your head that you might be wrong? That there might be some other explanation than the one you've given yourself?'

His grip tightened cruelly, but she was too incensed to feel anything other than her surging anger merging with a peculiar pain. He wasn't the only one to have lost people he'd loved.

'I didn't need to give myself any explanations. At the time, they were all too damned obvious.' He shot back in a steely voice. 'I suppose your precious cousin told you some whitewash story——'

'Stuart told me nothing,' she broke in furiously. 'He said it was nobody's business but his and Shauna's ... and that if you'd rather go on believing an ugly lie about your own sister than listen to the truth then that was your affair.'

Jenna tensed herself, waiting for the anticipated explosion of wrath, but he seemed turned to stone, his granite face frozen into an expression of torment.

When he finally spoke, his voice was so low that she had to struggle to hear him.

'It's Anderson who's lying.' The words came with difficulty through stiff lips.

'Are you sure? Did you ever ask him what had happened between him and your sister?' she probed, quietly now.

Duncan shook his head, a look of confusion dawning on his face that made him seem vulnerable.

'Then how can he have lied,' Jenna insisted, 'when he's never said a word?'

He drew a deep, harsh breath and the look of vulnerability that had secretly touched Jenna's tender heart, vanished to be replaced by the familiar grimace of bitterness.

'He didn't have to. I could see that he was someone special to Shauna. He seems to have that effect on certain women.' He laughed, the harsh sound grating on Jenna's overstretched nerves. 'And, of course, he would find it easy to make you believe in him.'

'Only if he was telling the truth,' Jenna argued, with a return of her anger. 'Unlike you, the truth is all I'm interested in.'

'And are *you* sure of *that*?' He snorted derisively. 'Anderson's good-looking, I'll give him that. But I thought you capable of looking beneath the surface to the real personality.'

'You mean the way you do?' she bit back sarcastically. 'Forgive me if I find that amusing . . . coming from a man like you who is prepared to hold a vendetta against another man without ever having given him the chance to vindicate himself. Someone, moreover, who can allow that hatred to include innocent relatives of that man, however remote, and however young.' Her fury mounted as she thought of how her sister had come running to Duncan Fergusson.

'That isn't true.'

His hands were still on her shoulders and she could feel the steely hardness of his fingers biting into her flesh. She tried to wrench herself free, but he went on holding her.

'Isn't it?' she cried. 'Then why have you inveigled Suzie here on some pretext of having something to show her?'

'I didn't inveigle her,' he denied. 'I did have something I wanted her particularly to see. But I didn't tell her. I suppose it's possible Alex may have mentioned it.'

'On your instructions?'

'I won't even answer that.'

'So! What is this "something special"?' She challenged.

His gaze moved away from her face to some point over her shoulder. She turned to see Suzie standing at the door of the stables.

'Oh, Jenna! Come and see!' she called. 'Duncan has a new black horse. He's absolutely beautiful.'

Jenna wondered, with a stab of remorse, whether the child had been silent witness to the quarrel that had raged between her and Duncan.

He released his hold on Jenna, as though he too was disconcerted by Suzie's unnoticed presence.

'I...I would like to, pet,' she said in a cracked voice. 'But I thought you wanted to see the fête.' Her desperate gaze saw people beginning to gather in the top field. 'It looks as though they're starting.'

'Yes, I know, but couldn't we stay just a little longer? Don't you want to see Midnight Satin?' A look of pride took the place of uncertainty, on Suzie's small face. 'Duncan said I could name him and I thought of that one myself. He's so beautiful,' she went on coaxingly. 'I'm sure you'll love him.'

And as Jenna stood rooted to the spot, while she struggled for some way out of her dilemma, her eyes went to Duncan's face. He was watching with a frown between his dark brows, obviously waiting for the outcome of her inner battle.

When she continued to stand irresolutely, he took her elbow.

'Perhaps Jenna could manage a minute or two, just to take a look.'

'Oh, great!' Suzie rushed over to take his free hand and almost dragged them both back to the stable, where the young horse stood a little restlessly.

'There! Isn't he the most beautiful horse in the world?'

Jenna couldn't help melting a little at the happy note of pride in her sister's voice. And she couldn't deny Midnight Satin certainly was a beauty.

'He's lovely.'

Suzie prattled on happily. 'Duncan said he would help me learn to ride him. And Duncan said I could come over any time to groom him and take care of him . . .'

'Duncan's said a lot of things, it seems,' Jenna broke in, her bitterness returning, before she had a chance to curb it. She softened her voice and went on. 'But he doesn't understand that we'll be leaving here before long.'

'Why do we have to?' Suzie's chin turned mulish. 'I like it better here.'

With Duncan's dark, deliberately expressionless eyes pinned steadily on her face, Jenna had to struggle even harder to hide her irritation. Just by saying nothing, he was piling on the pressure.

'We have a home of our own, Suzie,' she said as reasonably as she could manage. 'I have to pay the rent and I can't do that without a job. I have to go back to find another one.'

'You've lost your job?' Duncan cut in, finding his voice at last, it seemed.

'Yes,' she answered him woodenly. 'The school I taught at had to take a government cut in finances, and, as last in, I was the obvious choice for first out.'

It was ridiculous, but she felt she had to make the explanation because she didn't want him thinking she'd been sacked for incompetence. *What does it matter what he thinks?* a protesting voice cried within her, but she knew it did matter.

He moved close to Jenna, bending his head so that his mouth almost touched her ear. The warmth of his breath tickling against her skin sent a *frisson* of excitement shooting up her spine, making her stiffen with reaction. She tried to move away, but his arm hooked about her shoulder to hold her still.

'If you married me, it would solve all your problems.'

As much as she hated him this near, Jenna was grateful the whisper hadn't carried to Suzie's finely tuned ears.

'The answer would still be no, if my problems were multiplied by ten,' she hissed.

Suzie was rapt, her small hands delightedly stroking the rich black coat of the horse, and Duncan drew Jenna quietly away.

'Be reasonable, Jenna. At least let's talk about it.'

'What can you possibly say that I'd want to hear?' she said, fighting to keep her voice low. 'It's obvious you hate us all so much that you're capable even of hurting Suzie. Why else would you promise her what you have, knowing none of it is possible?'

'It is possible, and you know it,' he insisted, reaching for her hands, holding them against her attempts to snatch them away. 'If you'd marry me...'

She gave a short humourless laugh to cover the stab of pain which shot through her. 'How could I marry a man I didn't love?' she jeered, hating him for what he was doing to her heart.

He straightened his shoulders, but still held on to her hands. 'You may not love me,' he said tightly, 'but you want me. That at least I do know.'

'If it makes you feel any better to believe that, then go on believing it,' Jenna retorted, battling for her pride.

'I can prove it,' he said, a cynical smile curving his mouth, which looked suddenly cruel, as he reached out to draw her against him. 'Do you want me to do that?'

He was going to kiss her, and, despite everything, Jenna knew it was what she wanted more than anything, but it was madness.

'In front of Suzie?' she challenged derisively. 'Why not? One more disgusting scene couldn't do any more harm than the first, I'm sure.'

He groaned, his eyes flicking to Suzie, who was mercifully still engrossed. To Jenna's relief, he released his hold on her.

'There will be other times,' he said, his voice low and hard. 'Then we'll see.'

Jenna didn't bother to argue. All she wanted to do was put as much distance as was possible between herself and this hard, ruthless man, whom, inexplicably, she found so irresistible.

She broke away from him and went to Suzie, aware that her breath was ragged in her throat. She took a deep breath to steady herself, before saying, 'If you're ready, then, Suzie, we'd better take a look at this fête before it's finished.'

With one last, longing look at Midnight Satin, Suzie allowed herself to be led away.

CHAPTER NINE

JENNA pulled her cardigan more closely around her shoulders. A stiff breeze had blown up, and was cutting through her clothes. Clouds were gathering on the horizon and there was an acid tang in the air which foretold a storm. She ought to turn back, but the thought of putting on a cheerful face, pretending she wasn't eating her heart out, was more than she could bear.

It was Sunday, and there was no riding-school work to absorb her thoughts and energy. She'd managed to help Louise prepare the lunch with a certain amount of composure, but when Stuart had offered to help her with her self-imposed task of washing-up that composure had begun to crack. He'd seemed bent on trying to tease her out of her depression, but it had only made matters worse.

Pleading a headache, she'd managed to get out of the house.

Now she was alone on the empty road, her mind kept circling back to Duncan. Seeing him again had brought back all the old confusion of feeling. He was right—she wanted him. The question of why that should be so was unanswerable. She just had to accept that he seemed to hold some peculiar fascination for her.

Perhaps the only way she would be safe from his magnetism was to leave Glenrae. Simply to take Suzie and go. But that would be far easier said than done at the present. Her sister was still brooding on what she saw as Jenna's unreasonable refusal to stay. To her innocent mind, it must seem she was being deliberately denied access to Duncan's friendship and the young black horse she'd named Midnight Satin.

She sighed with frustration. Nothing was simple or straightforward any more.

It was growing darker by the minute and Jenna looked up at the lowering sky as a large spot of moisture struck her forehead. The downpour which, a few minutes ago, had seemed miles away, was now imminent, she realised irritably, and she would have to find somewhere to shelter if she wasn't to be soaked to the skin.

To the right was the side-road which led to the old wood, and Jenna remembered the forlorn-looking cottage. Perhaps she could ask for shelter there until the storm blew over.

She draped her cardigan over her head and shoulders as the rain started to fall in earnest, and began to run. The track was rutted and uneven and the windows of the cottage had a blank, unwelcoming look. It wasn't until she arrived, panting with exertion, that she realised it was uninhabited.

The front door wasn't locked. Hesitantly, she pushed it open and stepped inside. There was no hallway. The entrance led directly into the tiny living-room. The furniture which still remained was hung with cobwebs and the half-burned logs of a long-extinguished fire lay in the grate.

The atmosphere was a trifle eerie, as though past inhabitants had one day simply disappeared, never to return.

Jenna shrugged off such fanciful notions. At least inside it was dry, safe from the torrential rain which beat noisily at the slated roof.

Her cardigan was damp but still wearable and she put it on again, wrapping it around her, rubbing at her arms to warm herself up. It seemed colder inside than it had been outside and she looked at the logs, wondering if it would be possible to re-ignite them into a fire.

For the first time in days, her mind was diverted to something other than Duncan, as she allowed her curiosity to take her all over the cottage. It was small, but very comfortable, the furniture dating back, probably, to the turn of the century, with a marble-topped wash-stand in a corner of the one double bedroom. A feather mattress with heavy linen sheets and faded patchwork quilt were still on the bed and Jenna wondered about its last occupant.

The noise of the rain on the roof was deafening as she made her way down the narrow, steep stairs. It smothered the sound of her shocked scream as a dark figure suddenly loomed before her.

Her fear was in no way diminished as she recognised the grim, unsmiling face which met her horrified gaze.

'You . . . you frightened me,' she gasped at last, managing to tear her eyes away from his narrowed stare and to take the last few steps to the ground.

'What are you doing here?' Duncan Fergusson demanded.

Jenna stared back at him. 'I'd have thought that was obvious. I'm sheltering from the storm.'

His expression remained stony, impassive.

'I was curious, so I took a look around.' She moved past him. 'The owner's not here to mind.'

'Curiosity seems to be a prominent feature of your personality.'

He followed her into the small living-room, his broad bulk seeming to fill all the space around them.

'And you're wrong. The owner is here, and perhaps he does mind.'

Jenna looked quickly around at him.

'You? You own this house?'

'Yes. It's part of my estate.'

She laughed mirthlessly. It wasn't that much of a surprise. 'If I'd known I would have given it a wide berth and put up with a soaking.'

'Then you'd have been a fool.'

He moved towards her and Jenna shrank from him, but he went past her to the grate.

'Are you wet?'

'Just a little. I ran for cover before it became really heavy.'

'I wasn't so lucky.' He knelt on the hearthrug. 'Let's see if we can get this fire going. I need to dry my clothes.'

Jenna stood back, watching him as he found newspaper and kindling, and set it alight beneath the charred logs, her eyes following every movement, mesmerised by the strong play of his muscles beneath his wet shirt. The sight excited her, despite her attempts to distance herself from him.

'As soon as the rain stops, I'll leave,' she said, and it sounded like a vow. She was disgusted to realise that her voice wobbled almost as much as her knees.

'In that case, make yourself comfortable,' he said drily, his attention still concentrated on making the logs catch flame. 'The storm will last for hours yet.'

Jenna groaned inwardly. The question was, could she last out for hours? If he came to her...if he touched her...she wouldn't last five minutes.

'What are you doing out alone in the rain, anyway?' He turned his head and gave her a cynical look. 'Nothing at home to keep you amused?'

Jenna ran her tongue around her dry lips. She didn't want to quarrel with him again today, but it looked as though she might be forced to.

'I had a headache,' she said tightly. 'Not that it's any of your business.'

'You're trespassing on my property and that's my business.'

'Well, I didn't know that at the time,' she argued, adding with mocking softness, 'Do you want me to apologise?'

He laughed shortly. 'That depends on how you intend to do it.'

'Quite frankly, I don't.'

To her surprise he laughed. 'It follows.'

Jenna shivered. The damp had seeped through her clothes making her feel chilly.

He gave her an assessing glance.

'I'll have this fire roaring up the chimney soon. Then you can take off those wet clothes and dry them.'

'No, thanks,' she replied derisively. 'I'd rather stay damp.'

'Suit yourself. Fortunately I'm not such a prude.'

He gave a grunt of satisfaction as the logs ignited and began to crackle. He stood up and, without a glance in her direction, began to strip off his wet shirt, revealing a tanned, muscular chest lightly covered with curling dark hair.

Jenna swallowed and closed her eyes to shut out the compelling vision and squeaked as she opened them again to find he was unzipping his breeches.

He paused and threw a mocking glance at her as he hung his clothes on a line strung across the wide fireplace.

'I'm afraid your maidenly modesty will have to take second place to any risk of my catching pneumonia.'

Jenna's gaze was riveted on the firm, supple strength of his legs and the hot colour ran in her cheeks as her eyes moved upwards to the narrow briefs, which could do nothing to hide his undoubted masculinity.

'You're enjoying this, aren't you?' she grated.

'Not as much as I might be,' he admitted pleasantly. 'But I think a hot bath might improve matters.'

Jenna laughed shortly. 'I don't think this place runs to such luxuries.'

'That's where you're wrong.'

Jenna watched in astonishment as he put his boots back on, still clad only in his briefs.

'If that's meant to be a turn-on,' Jenna remarked wryly, 'then I'm afraid it's more laughable than exciting.'

He opened the front door. 'I'll be back.'

'I can't wait,' Jenna said, wondering what on earth was coming next.

She watched in astonishment as he dived out of the front door into the rain and came back with a tin bath over his head and a metal bucket hanging from each arm. He dropped the bath in front of the fireplace and took the buckets to the sink, filled them with water and hung them on hooks suspended over the brightly burning logs.

'Have a seat.' He indicated a wooden settle to one side. 'This won't take long.'

She stared at him in silent astonishment and he laughed.

'Hardly the Ritz. But I come here sometimes when I've been hunting. I spend the night now and again just to air the place out or when I have an urge to get back to grass roots.'

'Surprising,' she murmured cynically. 'I got the impression you enjoyed the life of a laird.'

He nodded amicably. 'Oh, I do. But, at times, the simple life has strong appeal.'

And, as Jenna continued to stand, he pushed her none too gently into the settle and brought the bath in front of the fire. With the tip of one finger he tested the water in the buckets.

'Won't be long.'

After five minutes or so, he wrapped a rag around a handle of one of the buckets and lifted it off the hook, pouring the steaming water into the bath; then he did the same with the other.

'A little cold water now,' he mused. 'And the temperature will be perfect.' He raised an enquiring eyebrow. 'Would you care to join me?'

'Thanks, but I'm happy where I am.'

'Ah, good. Then you'll get a ringside seat.'

He laughed as her mouth opened in sudden realisation, and put his hands to the band of his briefs.

'Always the gentleman.' Jenna stood up in sharp annoyance and turned away in an attempt to hide the pounding of her heart . . . the racing of her pulse.

'Not always. Sometimes I can't help myself.' His voice was a soft taunt and too late Jenna realised her mistake in turning her back on him.

His arms came about her from behind, pinning her arms against her sides and pulling her back against him. She struggled, but he only held her tighter, his face against her hair, his breath caressing her cheek, his lips close to her ear.

'Getting back to the subject of a suitable apology,' he murmured, 'we're alone, Jenna, and I want you.'

Jenna gasped, suddenly apprehensive. He was right. They were alone, isolated as much by the unrelenting curtain of rain as by the geography of the cottage. If she screamed, no one would hear. She was helpless and he knew it.

'Even Duncan Fergusson doesn't always get what he wants,' she said defiantly.

Her hands plucked at his arms in a futile attempt to loosen his hold, but the touch of his warm skin only kindled the flame that had begun to spark in her.

'Let me go,' she said fiercely, kicking her heels back fiercely against his shins, but his steely muscles were forcing the breath from her body, weakening her resistance until she subsided with a whimper of despair.

'Kiss me, Jenna,' he commanded. 'Prove to me that you don't want me.'

Jenna knew that if she kissed him she would prove no such thing. Already her body was betraying her; already the searing tide of passion had begun to rise and soon she would have no will to resist.

'I don't have to prove anything to you,' she cried desperately. 'And it doesn't say much for your magnetism that you have to force a woman to kiss you.'

'Who said anything about forcing.'

In one swift movement, he spun her around to face him and as her gaze focused dizzily she saw the burning eyes grow dark with menace.

She tried to push him away, but she might just as well have been trying to push down a brick wall. Her strength ebbed swiftly, leaving her limp in his grasp.

'That's better,' he said softly, acknowledging her defeat. 'Why fight the inevitable?'

His lips claimed hers suddenly and, to her surprise, with tenderness. This was no brutal assault, but a deep, sweetly persuasive possession. His arms held her firmly, but without force, against his naked chest, where her fingers felt the warm, smooth skin, alive with an electric current which transmitted itself to her body as a surge of desire for even closer contact with him.

Against her will, her lips answered his with her own burning need, relishing the honey-sweet taste of him, acknowledging her starvation...the famine of the past weeks.

He was right. Why fight the inevitable? Why not take what was hers for the moment...a moment she could relive long after the equally inevitable cold awakening?

She shivered and he drew her closer, into the warmth of his embrace, his mouth increasing its demand, his tongue probing into silken secret corners. His hands moved the length of her spine, moulding her hips, arousing exquisite sensations, making her aware of his own arousal.

Somehow, she managed to drag her lips from his.

'Your bathwater is getting cold,' she muttered huskily.

'*Our* bathwater.'

His hands slid the cardigan from her shoulders and he brought his lips to the hollow of her throat as his fingers unfastened the buttons of her dress. It slipped away from her with a sighing sound that was echoed somewhere deep inside Jenna. She barely felt the removal of her slip and panties.

She was mad...mad...to let this go on!

He was kissing her again, naked flesh searing naked flesh, creating sensations that roared through her, rocking the foundations beneath her feet.

He lifted her, holding her up in his arms, lips still locked in an ecstatic kiss. She could have pulled her mouth from his now, but instead she wrapped her arms about his neck, her fingers in the thick, springy hair, deepening the kiss, holding him captive to her lips as he had held her.

He moved and she felt the warm silk of water against her feet as he lowered her gently. Then he was in the bath with her, urging her down into the water. With her eyes still closed, and his mouth on hers, she felt the movement of his soapy hands on her body, an exquisite sensation that made her squirm.

He stopped kissing her to laugh softly and she opened her eyes to look into his face, which had lost its hard lines and wore, instead, a tender smile.

'More, Jenna?'

She shuddered visibly and he laughed again.

'I take it that means yes?'

He dipped his hands into the water and lathered them.

'Where would you like me to start?'

She gasped at the touch of his hands against her throat. He leaned forward to kiss her, stroking down across her shoulders and down again to her breasts, making her shudder again with delight.

He found the soap again and put it into her hands. 'I like it too, Jenna.'

Shyly, at first, she began to stroke him and then, with gathering courage, as he groaned his pleasure, his own hands massaging more urgently against her skin, arousing her, in turn, to her own kind of ecstasy.

Then, as though he could bear her touch no longer, he grasped her wrists and pulled away.

Jenna opened her eyes and stared dazedly at him as he sluiced the soap from her body and then from his own. He stood up, pulling her up with him, wrapping her in a towel he'd hung from the line stretched across the fireplace.

He rubbed the moisture gently from her body and then briskly from his own, then he lifted her from the bath and seated her on the settle to dry her feet.

'Duncan...' she began to protest, but he silenced her with a kiss.

'Hush, my sweet.'

He was lifting her again, moving up the stairs, holding her as though she weighed no more than a feather.

Then Jenna felt the coolness of the coverlet against her back, stark contrast to the heat within her.

Duncan lay alongside her, his lips brushing her cheeks, her lids, the arched column of her throat, his hand stroking along her body, fleeting across her breasts and down over the sensitive skin of her stomach, fingers tangling gently in the fine curling hairs.

Jenna gasped, as every new sensation washed over her, and he lifted his head briefly so that he could look down into her wondering face. She saw the excitement in him, the gleam in his eyes that might be an answering wonder... or triumph...

'Now tell me you don't want me, Jenna,' he commanded in an urgent whisper.

A cold shadow fell between them.

How much did she want these memories? she asked herself. Enough to allow him this victory over her? Enough to let him make a prisoner of her own heart? Because, once she had tasted the final fulfilment of her body's need of him, she knew no other would ever satisfy.

And there was another need, deep within her, to transmit her love to him, to have him answer her with his. But that was an impossible dream.

'Duncan.' His name was torn from her lips. A plea for his understanding... for some sign that he knew what he was doing to her... making her a traitor to herself.

'Second thoughts, Jenna?' He smiled, a sardonic lift of the corners of his mouth. 'Too late, my sweet. Your wild little heart is beating for me.'

His fingers traced the shape of a heart across her breasts, and, before she could protest, he had traced it again with his lips, scorching her with licks of flame, branding her with an exultant declaration of possession.

'You're mine, Jenna,' he murmured against her melting skin. 'Deny it with words, but your body doesn't lie.'

She couldn't deny it. Not with her lips, as his mouth swiftly covered them, nor with her body, which welcomed him anew as he claimed her.

Overhead, the storm reached a crescendo, lightning penetrating the room with brilliant, seeking intent, thunder crashing behind like some chariot of vengeance, becoming absorbed into the thundering of her heartbeat.

Duncan was sleeping on his back, his body deeply relaxed, powerful arms flung above his head in the guileless posture of a child.

Jenna lay beside him, listening to the rhythmic sighing of his breath, watching the rise and fall of his tightly muscled chest and fighting the urge to run her fingers over the contours of his strong face. His lips were smiling and, for once, the grim lines from nose to mouth were ironed out, leaving his cheeks smooth except for the dark stubble which had begun on his chin. He looked young and strangely carefree.

In contrast, Jenna was filled with tension. He'd won and it was useless to regret what couldn't be altered. But she couldn't help wondering what would be the outcome of her mindless folly.

Duncan had taken his revenge . . . his dark mission accomplished. What now? Would he be content? Or was he, even now, dreaming of some new torture?

She groaned softly, and lay back, her eyes searching the yellowed ceiling for answers. What more exquisite torture could there be beyond that which she had just endured? To be loved by him, shown the heights to which he could lift her heart and the depths into which she would now undoubtedly plunge. To go on giving love in return for hate. To live each day knowing what might have been hers.

Even now, as he slept, his magnetism drew her. She ached to hold him . . . to rouse him to her need . . . to have him enfold her within the charmed circle of his arms. If she stayed here beside him, she might not be able to fight the temptation to follow her desire.

In her weakness, she had let him take her, but there was still the lie that he had overpowered her to hide behind. If she touched him now, provoked him into taking her again, as she desperately wanted him to do, there would be nowhere to hide. He would know how completely she was in his power.

Futile tears pressed against her lids as she looked into the bleakness of her future without him.

Cautiously, she slid from the bed, shivering as the cold air met her naked skin. From the little window, she could see that the storm had abated and the sun was shedding a watery light across the drenched landscape. But the storm in her heart still raged. She could run from the man still sleeping in the bed, but she knew she could never run from herself.

Her clothes were strewn about the living-room. The sight brought a flush to her cheeks, reviving, as it did the memory of her abandon. Hurriedly, she dressed, suddenly apprehensive that Duncan would wake and come looking for her. Pushing her feet into her damp shoes, she left the house.

She heard the impatient whinny of his horse from the old, weathered stable, and wondered if he'd heard it too. On feet winged with urgency, she fled.

CHAPTER TEN

STUART came into the office, where Jenna sat hunched over the accounts.

'When Louise asked you to help out, she didn't intend for you to work yourself to death,' he said irritably, startling her into looking up.

Jenna sighed wearily. Putting down her pen, she stretched her aching back.

'It's got to be done. If I leave it, it only piles up.'

He looked down at her, his smile, for once, absent.

'What's bothering you, Jenna? I wish you'd talk about it.'

Her gaze slewed away from him. She was tempted to deny there was anything wrong, to pass it off as tiredness, but somehow it seemed easier to be honest.

'It's nothing I can talk about, Stuart.'

'Not even to me?'

Jenna shook her head. 'Not even to you.'

Not even to herself, she thought in silent bitterness. She didn't want to remember. Remembering hurt. It brought back the memory of how she had last seen Duncan, sleeping like a child, oblivious to the raging torment he'd unleashed in her. The memories she had wanted to hoard against lonely nights were the demons that tore her apart making it impossible for her to sleep at nights or to find solace in the work of the day.

'It's Fergusson, isn't it?'

136

Stuart leaned forward and grasped her chin, pulling her up to face him. 'Jenna, what happened when you were at Fergusson's place? Did he take advantage of the situation to make love to you?'

He saw the answer in her eyes, reluctant though she was to give it.

'He did, didn't he?' His face suffused with colour. 'If I thought he'd——'

Jenna pulled her head back sharply. 'He didn't. Not then...' She caught herself up, on the point of revealing her deepest, darkest secret. 'It...it...wasn't like that.'

His brows rose and his mouth was a thin, hard line. 'Then what was it like?'

She shook her head, upset by his insistance. 'Please, Stuart. Can we drop the subject?'

Stuart's fists bunched, his cheeks fused with colour. 'If he hurt you in any way...I'll...'

She came quickly around the desk to stand before him. 'Oh, Stuart, he didn't.' Tears gleamed in her eyes. 'Can we drop it now? Please!'

Useless to talk, or even think about it now. Since that day in the wood, nearly two weeks ago, she had seen and heard nothing of him. It was foolish, but she had thought...hoped...prayed...

Stuart's eyes narrowed suspiciously, but then he relented with a sigh, and leaned towards her, his hands lightly on her shoulders, pressing his lips against her forehead.

'I'm sorry, Jenna. I didn't mean to upset you.' He rumpled her hair. 'How would it be if I made amends by taking you up to the loch?'

Jenna hesitated. She was hurting and yet was somehow reluctant to relinquish her suffering. Locked

away here in the office, her conscious mind wrestling
with the problems of mundane administration, that
suffering was a physical and mental reminder that
Duncan had been her lover, however briefly. Her
memories were torture, unbearable torment, but they
were the only link she had with him. But she couldn't
stay tied to them forever.

'OK,' she said with deliberate lightness. 'You're on.'

Picking Suzie up from the stables on the way out,
they rode their horses at a leisurely pace across miles
of open land towards the gleaming waters of the loch.

Later, as Jenna sat with Stuart, watching Suzie
poking about in rock pools, he captured her face and
gave her a searching look.

'If it isn't Fergusson, then what's making you unhappy, Jenna?'

Jenna sighed. Apparently, he hadn't really given up.

'I'm not unhappy.'

It was a lie and they both knew it. She flushed beneath his penetrating gaze.

'You look very much like someone who's loved and
lost,' he said gently. 'I recognise the expression, having
seen it often enough in my mirror.'

Jenna looked at him in sudden understanding, and
her eyes were soft with sympathy. 'Oh, Stuart! Were
you in love with Shauna?'

It seemed suddenly like the right moment to ask.

'Yes.' He sighed. 'Unfortunately, the feeling wasn't
mutual. She was in love with her husband. He trav-
elled a lot with his job, sometimes for months on end,
and when he was away she stayed in Glenrae.' He
sighed and looked away, as though gazing into the
past.

Then he went on. 'She was lonely, so she turned to me as a friend. From her point of view, that's all it was—friendship. Bad luck it wasn't the same for me.' He grimaced. 'That's why I left and went to Edinburgh. Seeing her so often ... knowing I didn't have a chance ... it hurt.'

'But Duncan thinks she went after you. Do you think she missed you after you'd left and realised she loved you after all?'

'Never in a million years. It was her husband she loved.' He gave a sad little laugh. 'They had a small flat in Edinburgh. I assume she was going there to wait for him. She never did love Glenrae the way Fergusson does. Perhaps that's what he finds hard to accept.'

Jenna suddenly remembered Duncan's face when she'd admired his house. Remembered too his subtly caustic remarks about Jenna not loving it so much if she had to live there. Had he been referring obliquely to Shauna? Had he, after all, had some idea of what his sister had been suffering, separated from her husband, and hating Glenrae because it added to the distance that kept them apart?

She wished it were possible somehow to bring together the two men who had loved Shauna Fergusson, to talk about their grief, but she knew it was hopeless.

'Does it still hurt?' she asked Stuart sympathetically.

He grinned lop-sidedly. 'I haven't been looking in the mirror much lately. I've been too busy looking at you.'

She shot him a quick glance, expecting to see the usual teasing glint in his eye. But he seemed quite serious.

He took her hand and squeezed it. 'I'm glad you came to Glenrae.'

'So am I,' she agreed—a little guardedly, but it was true. Bitter-sweet as the past few weeks had been, she couldn't wish they had never been. 'But I'll soon have to start thinking of going back home. I have to do something about finding another job.'

'You've got a job, right here.'

'Only for the summer,' she protested. 'Later, it will be less busy and you won't need me.' She snorted gently. 'Besides, Marianne will be more comfortable when I've gone. I have a sneaking feeling I'm the reason she isn't around much at the school.'

He grinned. 'You may be right. Marianne never could stand competition. But if it's Marianne you're worrying about, don't. She's talking about selling up her half of the business.'

Jenna felt a jolt of surprise. 'But why?'

He shrugged. 'Who knows? But she hinted that Fergusson might be going to make an honest woman of her at last.'

The blood drained so quickly from Jenna's face that it left her nauseous. Fortunately, Stuart wasn't looking at her at that moment and she was able to pull herself together sufficiently to ask, with only the slightest tremble in her voice. 'You...you...mean they're going to get...married?'

He laughed. 'That's the impression I got. I'm not really too surprised. It's been on the cards for some time—at least as far as Marianne is concerned. Perhaps Fergusson thinks it's time to give in. He knows Marianne always gets what she wants...in the end.'

It was hard to keep her face from crumpling; even harder to hide the trembling of her hands. She looked away from him to where the sky met the horizon across the shimmering loch. The scene was so beautiful that it hurt almost too much to look at it, the pain mingling with a greater pain. Duncan had taken his revenge . . . his pound of quivering willing flesh . . . and set himself free.

It didn't matter to him that, in doing so, he'd made her a prisoner for life.

Suzie still pottered about among the rocks, totally absorbed in her peaceful preoccupation, a startling contrast to the turmoil of Jenna's reeling mind.

There could be no doubting now that Duncan had had no intention of ever marrying Jenna. His proposal really had been another of his cruel hoaxes, designed to humiliate and torture the cousin of the man he hated. If she had withstood him in the cottage, would he have had to go on with the sham?

Up until now, she had put off thinking about the future. Despite her words to Stuart about looking for a job, she couldn't really imagine her life away from this place . . . these people. Somewhere at the back of her mind had lurked the stubborn hope that perhaps . . . But she realised now how foolish that hope had been.

She swallowed hard, willing herself to appear unperturbed. 'What will you do if Marianne sells up and leaves?'

He turned to her with a strange, half-humorous expression on his face. 'I don't know. I suppose I'll buy Marianne out and run the school with the help of someone competent.' His eyes held hers. 'How do you feel about applying for the job.'

Jenna felt as though the breath had been knocked from her body. She stared at him, wondering if he was really serious.

'So, what do you think, Jenna? Are you interested?'

Still floundering under the weight of his revelation about Marianne and Duncan, and his unexpected offer, Jenna could only shake her head.

'Oh, Stuart,' she whispered at last. 'I can't.'

It would be impossible, to go on living in Glenrae, with Duncan only a few miles away, married to Marianne.

'Or won't,' Stuart said a little curtly.

'Don't, Stuart, please.'

She was close to tears and he looked into her face with sudden understanding.

'Oh, you poor sweet fool,' he said softly. 'So it's Fergusson after all.' He gave a short little laugh. 'Well, there's always me as second-best ... if you're interested.'

Her eyes widened in surprise and he shook his head in mock sorrow.

'I can see the thought never crossed your mind.' His eyes clouded. 'Pity. We might have been good for one another.'

Jenna shuddered, wishing with all her heart that it was possible to feel something more for him than cousinly affection ... possible for them to help each other to lay the ghosts of unrequited love. It would solve so many problems—for him, and for herself, and for Suzie.

'Oh, Stuart. You deserve more than second-best.' She put her arms about his neck and kissed him gently on the mouth. For a moment he held on to her, and then, with a little groan, he let her go.

'Is this a private party?' A cynical voice spoke from behind them. 'Or can anyone join in?'

Jenna recognised the dry tones of that voice and pulled herself from Stuart's arms with a startled gasp.

'Oh, please. Don't let us disturb you. Carry on.'

Jenna felt Stuart stiffen beside her and saw the gleam of fury in his blue eyes. She laid a restraining hand on his arm.

Her heart was pounding madly, leaping with sudden gladness that Duncan was here...even though he was looking down at her with a cold smile on his lips. She fought not to remember how sensuous those lips had been on hers...how tender...

'If you didn't wish to disturb us,' she said, with commendable coolness, 'why did you?'

The burning sensation in her cheeks increased as she felt the curious gaze of another pair of eyes— slanted, cat-green eyes which gleamed with malice. He had Marianne with him.

'I did tell you there was a little something going on there, darling,' she said sweetly. 'It's plain we're not wanted. Let's move on.'

She smiled seductively, one long pale hand spread elegantly against her beautifully curving hip.

Duncan glanced at her briefly. 'Have patience, Marianne,' he commanded. 'Do sit down.'

Stuart rose, despite Jenna's restraining hand.

'Can't you take a hint, Fergusson?'

Jenna stood up too, afraid of the electric tension sparking between the two men.

Duncan returned Stuart's stare.

'Don't worry, we won't stay long.' He turned his attention to Jenna. 'Where's Suzie?'

Startled by the unexpected question, Jenna pointed to where her sister sat hunched on a rock.

'Hunting for crabs.'

As they watched, the little girl dipped her hand into the water and surveyed her catch with obvious excitement.

'Looks like she's found something.' Duncan gripped Jenna's arm. 'Let's go and take a look.'

'Take your time,' Marianne cut in sarcastically. 'I can wait.'

She subsided, with a look of annoyance, as she realised that no one was paying attention.

Stuart was looking at Jenna. 'You don't have to go with him,' he said, deceptively soft.

Suzie had spotted Duncan and waved excitedly. 'Come and look. It's a big one.'

Duncan said. 'Come on. Let's go.'

He looked grimly determined and Jenna had reason to know what that expression meant.

She gave Stuart a look that begged for understanding, before allowing Duncan to drag her off in the direction of the rocks.

Some distance away from the others, she shook herself free of him and demanded harshly. 'Why have you come here?'

He was indifferent to her anger. 'I came for a breath of fresh air. I didn't know you would be here.' His eyes searched hers intimately, sending a high voltage of electricity shooting through her body. 'But for once fate was on my side and saved me the trouble of seeking you out.'

She lifted her chin proudly, meeting his probing stare.

'Why should you want to do that?'

He brushed a strand of hair away from her face, his palm cupping her cheek momentarily.

'This Martin ... the man you were engaged to ... it wasn't serious, then?'

Jenna frowned, feeling a little chill beginning inside. Oh, lord! He knew!

'What do you mean?'

'You know what I mean,' he stated impatiently. 'You never slept with him?'

She answered, hotly defensive. 'No. You may think me old-fashioned, but I don't jump into bed ...' She stopped as she saw the look on his face, which somehow had her heart beating madly in her throat.

'Why did you run away from the cottage?' he asked softly. 'You should have stayed.'

'Why? To give you the chance to gloat?' She called up the last vestiges of her pride and tossed her head back out of his reach, afraid of the smallest physical contact between them. 'You got what you wanted. Wasn't that enough?'

He grunted impatiently. 'Not all that I wanted.'

Her eyes widened disbelievingly. 'You mean there was more?'

'A little.' He smiled coldly. 'I've asked you to marry me.'

Jenna couldn't believe her ears. So he still intended to go on with that farce. He'd taken all she had to give and yet still he wanted more ... in pain ... and suffering.

'And I gave you my answer,' she flared furiously. 'It was no.'

He moved suddenly forward, gripping her shoulders in steel-hard hands.

'Perhaps it *was* Anderson all along. Today isn't the first time I've seen you making love to him.'

Jenna stared at him, wracking her brain for his meaning. Then she remembered Stuart's light kiss the day they'd gone to the village.

'I wasn't making love...' she began, rising to his bait, but she was stopped by the sheer contempt in his eyes. 'Anyway, it's not your business.' Fury brought a sob to her throat. 'So kindly stop spying on me.'

His mouth curled. 'You can't call it spying, if you're shameless enough to make love in the open...'

Jenna wanted badly to strike him, but she said, 'We do it all the time,' adding perversely, 'It's hard to hide real love.'

'What would Anderson know about love?' He pulled her close in a swift movement that took her breath away. 'By the way, does he know he's too late? That you're already mine...?'

Jenna felt sick with outrage. He'd had his revenge, and now he wasn't above gloating.

'Remember, Jenna?' His voice was a sibilant whisper. 'I won't let you forget.'

His lips hovered over hers and she felt the pressure of his hard body against hers, sapping at her strength, but she couldn't let him win again.

'When Stuart makes love, he means it,' she spat the words at him. 'And I'm going to marry *him*.'

The words were out of her mouth almost of their own volition, filling her with dismay as she saw the terrible darkening of his eyes.

His hold on her slackened momentarily and she took advantage of it to escape him, standing back a little shakily to watch the play of emotions across his face. Love was close to hate and she found herself revelling in the pain his pride was undoubtedly causing him. She was panting as though with exertion, but knew she was ready for flight if he came for her.

But he didn't. He simply stood there, his hands hanging loosely by his sides, staring at her as though seeing a ghost.

'Over my dead body.'

His voice, low and icy cold, sent a shiver of apprehension through her.

'Why did you take so long?'

Suzie's breathless voice cut between them, slicing the atmosphere. 'I had a really big crab, but he got away.'

As though waking from a trance, Duncan shook his head and looked down at Suzie. Slowly, the colour returned to his cheeks and the tension eased out of his face.

'We were having an interesting discussion, your sister and I,' he said, chilling Jenna to the bone as he added. 'It isn't finished yet, but for now it can wait.'

His large hand ruffled Suzie's curls.

'How's Midnight Satin?' she breathed wistfully. 'Is he broken yet?'

'Not quite yet.'

Jenna was amazed at how ordinary his voice sounded now, with a warmth for her little sister that appeared amazingly sincere.

'But it won't be long.'

'When he's ready, can I ride him?'

'I don't see why not. As long as someone's around at the time to make sure you come to no harm.'

Stop it! Jenna cried, silently, because she was filled with a kind of agony. Was there no weapon he was unprepared to use against her?

'Can I come tomorrow?' Suzie asked, seeming unaware of the tension strung out between the two adults.

'That's a question you'd better ask your sister,' he said pleasantly. 'If she says yes, I'd be delighted to see you both.'

Jenna gasped audibly. How dared he drag Suzie into it? He knew only too well she would have no peace from the little girl if she refused to take her. She shot him a glare of pure hatred and he answered it with a calm smile.

Damn him! Damn him a thousand times!

'Oh, please, Jenna.' Suzie's face glowed up at her. 'Can we.'

'Can we talk about it later, Suzie?' she hedged desperately. There was no way she could willingly put herself at his mercy again.

'We could go tomorrow couldn't we?' Suzie insisted, her eyes still hopeful.

'Maybe.' Jenna's heart bled for her disappointment. 'If not tomorrow, then perhaps another time.'

She didn't like what she was doing ... giving Suzie hope ... but it was the only way, until she could try to find some explanation that would satisfy the little girl.

'Please, Jenna,' Suzie said again. 'I want to see Midnight.' She set her jaw in a gesture Jenna knew spelt trouble. 'If you won't take me, I'll go alone. Like I did last time.'

Jenna gasped.

'Suzie, listen to me. Last time you could have been killed.' Jenna knelt and drew her sister gently to her. 'I want you to promise me you'll never do anything as dangerous as that again.'

'I won't promise!' Suzie cried, red spots of temper burning in her cheeks. 'I want to learn to ride Midnight and you can't stop me.'

'Suzie, please,' she cried desperately.

But Suzie tore herself away and went running up the beach.

Jenna spun angrily on Duncan Fergusson, facing him with eyes that blazed. 'Do you see what you've done?'

His brows rose infuriatingly. 'Do you mean it's wrong to express pleasure at the thought of your company?'

'That's got nothing to do with it and you know it,' she gritted.

'Oh?' His brows rose quizzically. 'Then what has it to do with?'

'You know perfectly well. Do you think I don't?'

'I can't answer until you enlighten me with your version.'

Suddenly, from the corner of her eye, Jenna caught the movement of a white shirt and realised that Stuart was coming towards them. If they were quarrelling when he arrived, it might precipitate a fight between the two men.

She said in desperation. 'Have you caused damage enough? Or are there even lower depths to your character you want me to see?'

For an instant, his eyes flared, mirroring her own anger, but then he smiled thinly.

'There's a lot I wish you could see, Jenna,' he said tightly. 'But, as I said, it can wait.'

'That's OK! If you don't mind waiting forever.'

With that parting shot, she followed Suzie up the beach.

Stuart met her halfway and, on impulse, she reached up and kissed him, and had the satisfaction of seeing a deep scowl wipe away Duncan Fergusson's bland expression.

He left without another word to anyone, a disgruntled Marianne in tow, and Jenna found herself trembling from head to foot, unable to decide whether it was relief or dismay.

Suzie stared after Duncan with a look of longing, which turned to sullenness when Jenna unconsciously ruffled her hair to comfort her. Jenna did her best to coax her back to her cheerful self, but the little girl ignored all her efforts and it was obvious her sulks were going to last for some time.

As well as that discomfort, Jenna had to fight with her conscience. After his initial surprise, Stuart had returned her exuberant kiss, and she hoped fervently she hadn't raised any false hopes in him.

CHAPTER ELEVEN

JENNA woke the following morning with a dull headache and a feeling of fatigue. She'd spent a restless night trying to work out what she should do. Things were now, of course, complicated by Suzie's attachment to Glenrae and everything that went with it. Yesterday's scene at the beach hadn't exactly helped matters either.

At breakfast, her tentative suggestion to Suzie that they might both be happier if they went home brought a flood of tears.

'I don't want to go home. I'd rather stay here. You can't make me leave if I don't want to.'

Jenna bit her lip and cast a despairing look at her aunt. Louise's gently impartial shrug surprised Jenna, making her wonder if Louise knew about Stuart's offer of a job at the riding school and was adding her own subtle pressure to persuade Jenna to stay.

Stuart had left earlier to see to some business in the next town, which was, in a way, a relief. He'd had an unsettling light in his eye and it was obvious to Jenna that he'd been brooding about Duncan's intrusion into their day out yesterday. Jenna thanked goodness for his absence. If he'd been around to witness Suzie's mutiny, obviously brought on by Duncan, things might have become even more complicated.

'Jenna,' Suzie's piping voice broke into her thoughts, 'you're not listening to me. I said I don't see why we can't go to Duncan's today. You said we'd talk about it.'

'I know, pet,' Jenna soothed. 'But I really don't think we'll be able to make it today.'

There was an ominous silence, as Jenna waited for the tears to flow, but it seemed Suzie was too tough for such weakness today.

'Why do you hate Duncan so much?' she enquired coldly. 'He only wants to be our friend.'

Jenna gasped, feeling close to unaccountable tears herself. How did one explain to a six-year-old the ramifications of adult behaviour?

'I don't hate him,' she denied, knowing it was true. 'And I really would like to think he was our friend, but——'

'He is. You're just being horrid,' Suzie interrupted hotly. 'And I hate being your sister.'

She stood up and rushed from the breakfast table without finishing her porridge.

The two women looked at one another in silence.

'I hope she'll get over it,' Jenna said worriedly. 'I just didn't know how to explain that the hatred's on his side.'

Louise patted her hand understandingly. 'Don't worry, dear. It's probably just a storm in a teacup.'

I wish I could believe that, Jenna thought despondently.

She saw Suzie later at the stables, still looking stubbornly unhappy, but the little girl ignored her attempts at cheerful conversation.

Seeing the woeful little face, Jenna felt sad. After all, Suzie had had few occasions over the past year or so to be joyful and it was a pity to have to dampen her spirits now. But she was filled with apprehension, knowing Duncan's obsession and how far he was prepared to go to feed it. She had suffered at his hands and was terrified that Suzie too would be made to pay the price. She cursed him, even as she told herself he was incapable of being so cruel.

Later, in the office, she found some paperwork which should have gone to town with Stuart and which he'd obviously forgotten. She frowned; it wasn't of vital importance, but it did mean another trip would have to be taken and an inevitable delay in sorting the matter out.

On impulse, she decided she would take the papers herself. The trip by car would take her out of her dismal thoughts and could be used as a means of doing the same for Suzie.

'If you can go to town,' Suzie said resentfully, 'why can't we go to see Midnight?'

Jenna hid a sigh.

'This is very important business, Suzie,' she coaxed. 'It's something which has to be done, but we can turn it into fun. Once we're there, we might have time to look around, maybe have tea with ice-cream. Wouldn't you like that?'

Was it her imagination, Jenna wondered, or had Suzie's face brightened a fraction?

'Oh, come on, pet. Cheer up.'

Suzie said grudgingly, 'I suppose it might be fun.'

'That's my girl,' Jenna applauded, with a hug. 'Get your coat and let's go.'

But it seemed as though it was to be one of those days. Her car was playing up again, refusing to start first time and she had to go and find one of the stable lads to get it going.

'The firing's a bit uneven,' the lad told her casually. 'But it will be all right once the engine warms up.'

They set off eventually, but there didn't seem all that much power in the engine of the car as it trundled along the rutted side roads. She breathed a sigh of relief as they got out on to the wider road which went past Duncan Fergusson's estate.

Here the engine would get a chance to warm up as the lad had suggested.

But it was all wishful thinking. Two miles further on, the engine just cut out dead, and Jenna was forced to pull into the side of the road.

The weather was hot and sultry and, for once, the thin cool breeze which seemed to blow even on the hottest day was absent. Sitting in the car beside a disappointed Suzie, Jenna felt a longing to scream. It was pointless her getting out to look at the engine, since she didn't understand the first thing about them.

She looked about the deserted roadside, half expecting Duncan Fergusson to appear, as he had the first time they'd met with disaster in a car, but there wasn't a soul in sight. After nearly half an hour of sweltering in the car, with no sign of anyone, Jenna decided to walk. It was impossible to walk back to the school, so the only solution was to walk on.

'There's sure to be a house within walking distance,' she assured Suzie, hoping she didn't sound as doubtful as she felt. 'And they'll be bound to have a telephone. If we can't get a taxi, maybe someone at the school will come out to fetch us.'

They seemed to have trudged miles before the roof of a building came in sight.

'I told you we'd find somewhere.' Jenna quickened her step and then came to an abrupt halt as she recognised the distinctive tall chimneys.

Suzie recognised them at almost the same instant and perked up immediately. 'We're almost at Duncan's place,' she chirped happily. 'I knew I'd get there somehow.' She broke into a run.

Jenna, hurrying after her, cursed a seemingly malevolent fate, which appeared determined to deliver her into enemy hands.

'Suzie. Not so fast,' she cried breathlessly. 'Maybe there's somewhere else closer by.'

But there wasn't, she knew. The area surrounding the large estate went for miles before other houses appeared. The only exception was the little cottage near the wood, and even that was some distance away. Not that she wanted to go there. Even if it had been inhabited now, it would still be haunted by her bittersweet memories.

She caught herself up sharply. Her mind had been rambling, she knew, afraid to face up to the inevitable. She was going to have to ask Duncan Fergusson, once again, for help. With any luck, he wouldn't be there, and she could just ask one of his staff to drive her and Suzie back to the school. Stuart would no doubt pick up the car for her later.

But luck, as always, didn't seem to be working in her favour. As they approached the stables, Suzie still running on ahead, Duncan came out of one of the outbuildings.

He stood absolutely still for long seconds, then a smile broke on his ruggedly handsome features.

'Oh, good,' he said. 'So you made it after all.'

Suzie, after giving him a quick hug, rushed on past into the stables, undoubtedly to see her darling Midnight Satin, leaving Jenna alone to confront Duncan in the yard.

'This isn't a social visit,' she began awkwardly. 'My car has broken down, I'm afraid, and your place was the nearest one.'

He grinned sourly. 'Very graciously put, I must say. It's good to see you're on form.'

Jenna coloured. 'It wasn't meant to sound rude,' she said. Her voice sounded shaky because her heart was hammering at what felt like twice its normal speed. She took a deep breath, trying to steady it. Why was her response to him always so swift, so automatic and so uncomfortable? she wondered resentfully. 'The car really has broken down. It just stopped dead and refused to go on.'

His grin widened, and he looked almost pleasant. 'So magic does work, after all.'

'I'm half inclined to believe you would use black magic to get you what you wanted.'

'Not black magic,' he commented easily. 'A little white, perhaps. Come up to the house and I'll get one of the men to go and have a look at your car to see if it can't be rescued.' He came forward to take her elbow, but she moved it discreetly out of his reach.

'I'd be grateful if someone could. I'm going to town on some rather important business.'

'Sounds very high-powered,' he jeered mildly. 'You seem to have gone up in the world of big business.'

'Not at all.' Jenna coloured under his teasing. 'Even small businesses have some important things to attend to. We can't all be tycoons or landed gentry.'

'I'm sure,' he said solemnly, putting his hand in the small of her back to guide her towards the house. 'Meanwhile, let's go and see if Annie can rustle up some tea.'

Reluctantly, Jenna allowed herself to be led. There wasn't really any alternative other than to accept his hospitality, however much it hurt her pride.

She walked beside him in silence, as much from a nervous inability to open a conversation as from resentment of her situation.

'Are you sulking?' he demanded suddenly.

'Of course not,' she denied sweetly, with a barbed sidelong glance that belied her tone. 'It's very kind of you to rescue Suzie and me once again.'

He laughed amusedly. 'Don't mention it.'

It was the last time he spoke until they reached the house. It was agony for Jenna, walking beside him, her shoulder occasionally touching his, with the electricity running wild between them, and his face as expressionless as stone.

Annie was standing in the kitchen, as she had been the first time Jenna had come here, and she had to stifle a feeling of homecoming as the housekeeper came forward to give her a hug.

'It's nice to see ye again, dearie,' she said, her eyes going beyond Jenna searchingly. 'Is the wee girl with ye?'

'She is,' Duncan answered before Jenna could speak. 'But you've been replaced in her affections, I'm afraid. She's in the stables with Midnight.'

Annie smiled benevolently. 'Well, as long as she's happy.'

'Come through into the sitting-room.' Duncan took Jenna's elbow determinedly this time. 'Annie can fetch the tea through.'

Jenna set her lips, which inexplicably were trembling a little. She mustn't allow herself to feel there was any real welcome for her and Suzie in this house. If she didn't know it was impossible, she might almost suspect this scene had somehow been stage-managed . . . designed to cut away her resistance. But what would be the point? Now he was going to marry Marianne, surely Duncan didn't intend to go on trying to enact revenge from her? Despite her reasoning, a premonition of disaster forced itself into her awareness. She was convinced there was trouble to come.

It wasn't long before she knew she was right. Seated opposite to him, sipping at the refreshing tea Annie had brought, she felt the tension in him.

'If the car hadn't broken down,' he began, 'you wouldn't have come.'

'No. I wouldn't.'

He made an impatient sound and leaned towards her, an intense expression in his eyes. 'Why won't you even consider what I'm offering you? You love this place, you told me so once.'

Once, a lifetime ago. Jenna thought in silent bitterness.

'It's a wonderful house,' she conceded. 'In a wonderful part of the country, but——'

'Then let's start from there,' he said, his eye gleaming with a kind of fervour. 'Already Suzie thinks of this house as home.'

Jenna felt the kindling of the old anger. 'Yes, she does. With a lot of help from you, I suspect.'

He stared disconcertingly into her tight face. 'Always so suspicious, my little wild thing.' And, as she made no response to the warmth of his tone, he made a short impatient sound. 'Is it so hard for you to understand why I welcome Suzie here?'

Jenna stared back at him in disbelief. That he should ask for her understanding, when he gave none. Couldn't he see Suzie's love for him and his home was tearing the sisters apart? There was no way she could give her sister what her small heart desired, no matter how much it hurt them both not to.

'How could you?' she blazed. 'How dare you use Suzie in this way?'

His eyes gleamed, steely bright. 'What do you mean . . . use her?'

'You know exactly what I mean.' Her hand itched to hit the strong, cold face. 'You'd do *anything* to get back at Stuart Anderson, wouldn't you.'

His stony features paled. 'I won't deny I'd like to make him pay. His sort get away with things too often and too easily.'

Jenna stared at him, feeling impotent against his granite-hard resistance to reason.

'You don't know what really happened,' she said harshly. 'You don't *want* to know the truth.'

He stepped forward, looming menacingly, and took her shoulders in a hard grasp.

His lips curled disdainfully. 'Perhaps it's you who doesn't want to hear the truth.'

'What do you mean?' She twisted in his grasp, wrenching free with a cry of exasperation. 'None of this has anything to do with me, as I'm sure you must realise by now.'

He shook his head at her pityingly.

'Are you afraid your new-found love for your cousin won't stand up to knowing what he is . . . a womaniser . . . not above seducing another man's wife when his back is turned?'

Jenna froze, her eyes staring into his, with the memories flashing across, so clear that she felt he must see them too . . . feel the emotions that were raging through her.

She wanted to accuse him in turn. To cry 'Seducer . . . destroyer of dreams' . . . but it hurt too much.

At last, she said dully. 'It wasn't like that. Stuart loved Shauna.'

His body lost its nonchalant pose. His spine stiffened and his fists clenched whitely at his sides as though he had to keep them there, out of harm's way, or he would have struck her. His face suffused with startling colour.

'Do you dare delude yourself at my expense?' he gritted through clenched teeth. 'Do you dare mention Stuart Anderson's name in the same breath as love...in the same breath as *my sister*?'

Jenna gave a deep, despairing sigh. It seemed futile to argue against his grimly determined certainty.

'You're torturing yourself unnecessarily,' she insisted, despite her conviction that she was wasting her time. 'Shauna was never in love with Stuart. He went away to Edinburgh because he knew she would never love anyone but her husband.'

She saw the sudden stilling of his face, the slow clenching and unclenching of his hands and went on softly, 'It was only ever her husband she loved, and Stuart knew it.'

And now, for the first time, there was doubt in his eyes, a faint gleam of something that might be belief. A lump rose suddenly in her throat, and ached unbearably.

'If it wasn't for Anderson,' his eyes searched hers in bewilderment, 'then why was she leaving?'

Jenna shook her head gently. 'That's something perhaps only Shauna knows, unless in your heart you do.' She shrugged. 'Perhaps she wasn't happy in Glenrae.'

The sudden pained twisting of his mouth caught her by surprise.

As he came towards her, she drew back and stumbled. He caught her in his arms, drawing her close against him. But there was no tenderness in his hold, only cold, steely hardness, echoed in the vicious set of his jaw and the merciless piercing eyes that made her shiver.

'Are you trying to tell me I drove Shauna away?'

'That's not what I said,' she answered in dismay. 'Not what I meant at all.'

He jerked her convulsively tighter and she cried out in pain, but he seemed oblivious. 'Do you love him so much that you'd lie to me to protect him?'

'Let me go.' Her voice was a strangled gasp. 'You're hurting me.'

His answer was to sweep her up into his arms. Ignoring her struggles, he carried her past the open-mouthed Annie, who met them in the hall, and up the wide staircase to her old bedroom.

By then, she had ceased to struggle. Conflicting emotions warred in her. The feel of his arms around her brought back the racing excitement, the memory of another time when he had carried her, his lips locked on hers.

His face, so close to hers, was set aloof, frozen in fury. With her eyes level with the column of his strong throat, she saw the mad beat of his pulse in the hollow and longed, in wild desperation, to place her lips against it.

He kicked the bedroom door open, sending a juddering shock through her body. Marching across to the bed, he threw her roughly down on to the covers, the ice in his eyes replaced by a burning intensity.

'It's me you want, not Anderson, and we both know it,' he hissed. 'I won't let you throw yourself away on him, out of sheer wilful stubbornness. You will marry me, if I have to keep you here until you agree.'

Struggling up on to her elbow, she stared up at him, aghast.

'Don't be a fool, Duncan. You can't force me to marry you.'

His smile was grim. 'I'm hoping I won't have to.' He turned and headed for the door. 'A little time for reflection might be all that's necessary to persuade you.'

Before she had time to argue, he was gone, and she heard the rasp of the key turning in the lock. Seized by panic, she got off the bed and ran to the door, wrenching at the knob, knowing all the while that it was useless.

'Duncan!' she called, her voice a mixture of rage and pleading. 'Open the door.'

The sound of her voice seemed deadened against the heavy oak panelling of the door and she was filled with a sudden, ridiculous feeling that it was impenetrable; that she could shout forever and no one would hear her. She banged against it in desperation, calling to be let out, until her hand ached and her voice had faded to a hoarse whisper.

Where was Annie? she wondered. Was she part of this ridiculous fiasco? Whether yes or no, she wouldn't go against Duncan, Jenna knew.

There was no escape, she admitted hopelessly. Her shoulders drooped with fatigue and she stared dully around the room that had once seemed like home. Now it was a prison. Her heart ached. How easy it would be, in other circumstances, to think of this house as home. She sat on the bed, filled with sudden, exhausting weakness.

The panic was gone. Duncan couldn't keep them here for long. They would be missed. Surely, as time passed, her aunt would become anxious, ask questions, perhaps send out a search party who would see the stranded car and guess.

Her heart jerked with sudden tension. Suppose Stuart came here to look for her. The two men would meet in violence at last and God knew what the outcome would be. And she had unwittingly precipitated their confrontation... told Duncan a lie which had further embittered him against her cousin. Two men who hated each other, clashing over a woman they both professed to want. She suspected now that neither man loved her... each intent only on depriving the other.

Nothing made sense. She was supposedly here until she'd made up her mind to marry Duncan. Yet how could he still go on with that farce, when he was already planning to marry Marianne?

He must know Jenna loved him. He couldn't not know... not after her abandon in the cottage. Was he hoping to wring an admission from her as her final act of humiliation?

There was a coldness around her heart. If she'd thought herself unhappy in the past, it was nothing to the deep, despairing misery that filled her now.

That night in the garden, when he had first proposed, she had tried to persuade herself that she might succeed in teaching him to love her. What a fool she'd been... still was. Even now, if he were to come to her... to take her in his arms...

Despising her sudden weakness, she shook her thoughts away.

It was only a matter of time before Duncan returned to his senses and came to let her out, she told herself. He *had* to come. She couldn't bear to be cooped up here much longer. If he didn't come soon, she would go mad.

And where was Suzie. She was sure to ask after Jenna, and when she did, they would have to release her . . . wouldn't they?

She crossed to the door and rattled the knob, beating hard at the panel.

'Duncan!' she called. 'Let me out, please.'

But it was useless.

Pacing restlessly to the window, she looked out, hoping someone might see her, but the garden was empty. She opened the window, craning out for a view of the terrace, but her vision was obscured by the leafy branches of the tree which touched the wall beneath.

Her heart thudded. The tree was young, its branches not yet fully grown, but, with care, it presented an avenue of escape.

She tried to gauge the distance between the window and the nearest stout branch, hastily subduing a nervous tremor as she thrust one leg over the sill. It wasn't going to be easy.

But there was no point in dwelling on the difficulties. Best just to get on with it. She grasped a branch and brought her other leg over the sill, easing her feet into contact with the lower branch. It swayed as it took her weight. Slowly, with her heart in her mouth, she began to lower herself down, ignoring the discomfort of the short spiky branches which caught in her dress and in her hair, until she was jut ten feet from the ground.

It still seemed a long way down and dizzyingly difficult to reach the ground, but there could be no going back now. She had reached the point of no return in every sense.

Gingerly, shifting her weight, she slipped downwards until she was virtually hanging in the air. Holding her breath, she let go and, in the space of a second, fell into a strong pair of arms which gripped her like a vice.

'You fool,' growled a familiar voice. 'You might have broken your neck.'

For a moment, she was almost relieved. She had fallen into the arms of safety. But any illusion of safety was quickly dispelled as she looked up into his grim face and felt the steely hard restriction of his arms about her, which tightened at her tentative glance.

'Does Anderson mean so much to you that you'd break your neck to get back to him?'

Jenna's momentary feeling of euphoria vanished as she realised that, far from worrying about her safety, he was concerned only that she might be running from him into Stuart's waiting arms.

How he could possibly believe she might love Stuart after the way she had lain in his arms in the deserted cottage was impossible to imagine. Hatred, it seemed, overrode his perception and, with a sighing gesture of defeat, she acknowledged that it probably always would.

Despairingly, she tried to wrench herself free, but he held her fast, his fingers biting into the soft flesh of her upper arms as he shook her with a ferocity that made her head snap back.

'Answer me.'

Trapped and helpless, she wriggled in his grasp, her gaze locked tightly in his, searching hungrily, but having to concede that there was no tenderness anywhere in the dark depths.

With a feeling of jumping over a precipice, Jenna defied him.

'All right! Yes ... yes ... yes ... I want to go from here. To Stuart ... to Glenrae ... to anywhere away from you.' Her hard eyes challenged him. 'Is that what you want to hear?'

The hiss of his breath cleft the air between them, and his hold suddenly slackened. She had expected his answering fury, hard malice, anything but the stunned stillness of him.

Experience warned her that this moment of respite wouldn't last. Soon she would see the familiar change in him and then it would be too late.

With only the slightest of movements, she was out of his strangely nerveless hands and moving away. Somehow, her limbs had lost their iron weightiness and she was running from him, from herself ... from the future and what it might have been ...

She ran towards the stables, where she had left Suzie, rapt in the new acquisition. With that damned horse he had stolen Suzie's heart, which would break when they left for home. With a pain too deep to locate or rationalise, she damned him again and again for his cruelty.

Then, as she neared the stables, she saw a blur which clarified, as her eyes focused, into a prancing black beast with a small, determined figure astride its back.

She paused and then went forward slowly, hardly daring to breathe unless she startled the young animal.

Suzie saw her and called to her triumphantly. 'See. You couldn't stop me after all. I told you I'd ride Midnight, didn't I?'

Startled by her high-pitched voice, the horse began to snicker nervously.

Jenna halted, electrified with fright as she remembered Duncan's casual remark that the young animal wasn't fully broken.

'Yes, so you did,' she said, as calmly as she could. 'But, if I were you, I'd dismount now.'

'Just a couple more minutes,' Suzie coaxed. 'He doesn't mind. He likes me. Don't you, boy?'

She patted him on the neck and it was suddenly too much for the inexperienced horse. Before Jenna's horrified gaze, he broke into a jerky trot.

'Suzie! Stop!' The hoarse cry was torn from Jenna.

A startled, frightened little face turned in her direction and froze for a moment in time, before beast and child took off in a wild canter across the stable yard.

A hand caught at her arm and she looked up, horror-stricken, into Duncan's grim, shocked face.

Then, they were off together in a desperate sprint, Jenna almost level with him for the first hundred yards before, with long determined strides, he outstripped her.

'Suzie!' she screamed again, as she saw the flying leap which took the child over the fence and along the path towards the orchard.

'Suzie!' Duncan's voice swamped her own shrill cries. 'Pull him around. Don't let him into the orchard.'

Almost automatically, Jenna registered the speed and power of Duncan's muscular stride, which ate up the space between him and the small girl struggling to rein in her mount.

'Don't let him take the wall,' she heard him yell. 'Suzie, for God's sake! Draw in his head!'

Jenna's lungs were bursting, but she increased her speed, cutting through the orchard in a vain attempt to head Suzie off. Duncan, with the same idea, cut across from a different direction.

In a kind of slow motion, she saw Suzie shorten the rein and pull in the horse's head tight against its heaving chest, bringing it to a shuddering halt.

At that moment, she collided with Duncan, the force of the impact driving her breath from her body and sending her staggering against the low stone wall at the boundary of the orchard. For a few terrifying seconds, she saw the abyss beyond and then she was falling. The scream which formed in her throat died as someone grasped her ankles and jerked her backwards. She fell gasping into Duncan's arms, where he held her trembling against him.

She heard the high, crashing reverberations of his heartbeat and the thin rasp of his breath against her cheek. Close to, she saw the ashen pallor of his skin and felt his trembling. Their eyes met and she saw that his eyes were dark with emotion.

He pulled her convulsively against him, one hand sliding beneath her hair, the other about her waist as his lips pressed against the column of her throat. Her heart accelerated with sudden hope and her arms slid about him, feeling the hard, muscular strength of him, the warm comfort of his hold.

For a few seconds longer, he held her and she felt as though he would hold her forever, and sighed his name.

Then suddenly, he stirred, putting her from him abruptly, leaving her arms and her heart empty as she saw the renewed grimness of his expression.

'You little fool. You might both have been killed. Why didn't you leave it to me?'

He strode across to Suzie, who had, by now, clambered from her mount and stood, head lowered contritely, holding the reins of the gently snickering horse.

Duncan took them from her without a word and led the horse back towards the stable.

Jenna, almost unable to stand on her wobbly legs, went to Suzie and hugged her.

'Thank God you're safe!' she said devoutly. 'I might have lost you too.' Tears streamed down her face. She knew the vision of Suzie clinging desperately on to Midnight's back as he took the stableyard wall, would haunt her for a lifetime.

'Don't blame Midnight. It was all my fault.' The little girl began to cry, her small face puckered into so woeful an expression that it was almost comical.

'Don't cry, Suzie. All that matters is that you're safe.'

Jenna dabbed at her eyes with the back of her hand and stood up. She took the small hand in hers and led her sister back towards the house, where they waited in the front entrance until Duncan arrived with the Land Rover.

He came towards them and Jenna saw, with a sinking sensation, that the tight-closed expression was still in place. Waiting for him, she'd found herself hoping the drama might have pierced his perception, letting him see how much she loved and wanted him, but it hadn't happened.

His glance was almost impersonal as it flicked over her.

'Are you all right?'

She nodded. Somehow there seemed no point in words.

He didn't touch her, but his hand fell for an instant, in seeming forgiveness, upon Suzie's blonde curls.

'I'll take you back to the school.'

His voice was flat, empty of emotion.

In silence he lifted Suzie into the back of the vehicle before helping Jenna into the front seat. His fingers, brushing against the sensitive skin of her underarm, were icy cold, and she shivered, but not because of that. Somehow, he seemed to have abandoned her. It was almost as though he blamed her for what had happened and now it seemed he was willing to relinquish her, at last, to Stuart.

A sob rose in her throat but she smothered it.

He turned briefly in her direction, cool eyes piercing her defences. She turned away quickly, to peer blindly out of the window, willing herself not to cry.

At last, the Land Rover pulled up at the gates of the school.

Duncan held out his hand to Jenna to help her out, but she disdained it, knowing that if he touched her she would break down in tears. Pride kept her dry-eyed. She knew now, beyond a shadow of doubt, that all was finished between them. She couldn't pinpoint the moment when it had happened, she only knew that it had been inevitable.

She got out and watched as he lifted Suzie, holding her against him for a brief moment before putting her on to her feet.

The sadness in her sister's eyes cut Jenna like a knife.

In that moment, she hated him, and would have felt a grim satisfaction in telling him so, but held herself in check for Suzie's sake.

It was galling to realise that it wouldn't have mattered to him anyway. Having deposited them at the gates of the school, he climbed swiftly into the Land Rover and drove away, without even a backward glance, and no word of goodbye.

CHAPTER TWELVE

JENNA brushed her hair vigorously. In between strokes, she peered anxiously at her face in the dressing-table mirror. The healthy tan she'd acquired in the brisk Highland air had faded to a pale gold, beneath which her skin seemed drained and there were faint violet shadows beneath her eyes.

She sighed. This morning it was important that she look her best, at her most alert and self-confident. She had managed to get an interview at a primary school in a nearby town, but she was under no illusions about the kind of competition she would be facing.

She wished she could feel something more than apathy about the outcome. She ought to care, since, if she didn't get a job soon, things would become very difficult, but somehow it hardly seemed to matter.

Suzie's wan face was suddenly reflected in the mirror beside her own. Jenna felt the familiar pang at the lacklustre smile on her little face.

'I'm ready.'

Jenna hugged her, sighing as the small body stiffened. Suzie still hadn't forgiven her for dragging her away from the riding school, from Midnight, and from the people she'd learned to love. It hadn't been easy, but she'd hardened herself to all opposition. There was no way she could have stayed, knowing Duncan despised her.

Louise had cried, telling Jenna quite openly that she wished she'd stay and perhaps, in time, marry Stuart. So Marianne had been right after all.

Duncan still haunted her. Over two months had dragged slowly by and each day the hope that he might come grew fainter. She couldn't help wondering what would have happened if she'd accepted his proposal of marriage. It was a thought that cropped up in unguarded moments. She examined the thought gingerly, feeling a perverse kind of relief to realise that she didn't want him on those terms. Marriage to him in blind hope that one day he might love her would ultimately have destroyed her. This way, she at least still had her pride.

Putting down her brush, she stood up to examine her full-length view, noting dispassionately that she'd grown much thinner. Hollows moulded her delicate cheekbones and her businesslike suit hung straight and sleek about her dwindling curves.

Would Duncan be satisfied to know she was declining? she wondered cynically. Probably not. Having won his vendetta, he'd probably forgotten her, married Marianne and put the summer madness behind him. This too was a recurring thought which she used to test the pain, as one prodded an aching tooth to see if it had recovered.

The morning air was bright and clear, but with a forceful autumnal nip in the air, and Jenna was glad she'd worn her light wool coat. From the berries already clustering in red abundance on the holly tree in her small front garden, it was going to be a hard winter.

She wondered whether snow had already begun to fall in Glenrae and felt a painful desire to see the rugged beauty of the place blanketed in snow.

She left Suzie at the school gate, watching her reluctant trek up the gravel path, where she disappeared without even a backward glance at Jenna.

With a sigh, she turned away, deliberately directing her mind to her coming interview. She felt curiously detached and free from the characteristic nervousness of such an ordeal.

It was impossible to tell whether she'd made a favourable impression, she reflected after the interview, but at least they hadn't cut the interview short, which must hold out some hope.

She should have felt at least a little optimistic. Instead she felt curiously flat and weary as she turned the corner to home. At first, she didn't notice the Land Rover parked beyond the front gate. Then, in delayed reaction to the sight, her heart began to pound and then soar with hope. It couldn't be . . . and yet . . .

She was almost running by the time she'd reached the gate and collided with the man who was coming out. Her breath caught as hands clutched her and she looked up into a familiar smiling face.

'Stuart!' She half choked with disappointment. 'Wh . . . what are you doing here?'

'Paying you a visit, my sweet.' Stuart's smile was pained. 'You might at least pretend you're glad to see me.'

'Oh, Stuart.' Jenna's shrivelled heart expanded a little. 'I am glad to see you. You know I am.'

'Then prove it.' He kissed her lightly. 'I presume you're going to ask me in.'

When Suzie came home from school, she gave Stuart the kind of frenzied welcome he would have appreciated from Jenna. But her joy was short-lived once she realised he hadn't come to take her back to Glenrae.

Later, after Suzie had gone disconsolately to bed, Jenna sat with Stuart on the settee. Looking at his handsome face, she couldn't help wondering why she felt none of the sexual excitement Duncan's granite-hard looks aroused in her. Life would be so much simpler, she mused, if it were only possible to arrange such things in a conscious way.

She asked about Louise.

'Louise is fine, but told me to tell you she's missing you both very much.' He took her hand. 'Why don't you come back, Jenna? We really need you now that Marianne's gone.'

So Marianne had gone . . . to Duncan . . . ?

'It's no good, Stuart. Honestly.'

He frowned. 'No strings, Jenna. All I want is for you to be happy. And I think you *were* happy at Glenrae.' He was watching her closely. 'If you didn't fancy working at the riding school, there's a small local school in the village needing a teacher. A free cottage goes with it, so you won't have to see much of Louise and me if you don't want to.'

Jenna held back her tears. Oh, it wasn't fair. Just when she had almost begun to forget, he had to turn up, bringing with him all the pain and longing of her lost and lonely nights.

'I've already got a job,' she lied, putting a shaking hand to her hot cheeks. Seeing his disbelieving look, she confessed. 'Well, almost. I've had an interview anyway.'

He nodded.

'If it's Fergusson you're worried about, he's not around. Rumour has it he's gone back to Edinburgh to stay.'

Jenna blinked at him through tear-wet lashes, hardly daring to voice her heartbreaking suspicion. 'Did Marianne go with him?'

He shrugged. 'Who knows?'

Stuart stayed another two days, sleeping on the narrow bed in the spare room, and using every argument he could muster, but Jenna somehow managed to remain obdurate.

'Think about it,' he pleaded, as he kissed her goodbye. 'You're all the family Louise has now. She wants to see you happy. So do I.' He squeezed her hand. 'Come home, Jenna.'

Stuart's frown was thoughtful as he drove home. He was thinking about Duncan Fergusson, with all the bitter frustration of the past mingling with the present.

Damn the man. He appeared to be a magnet to young and beautiful women. Yet, by some strange quirk of nature, he seemed almost unaware of his impact. Marianne had driven off somewhere in a blind fury, and Jenna ... A picture rose in his mind of her face, hurting and vulnerable, her eyes dark pools of longing. A look it wasn't difficult to interpret. Was it really possible Fergusson didn't know?

Damn Fergusson, he cursed again, feeling his own grinding frustration bite deep.

Dust was falling as he rattled along the rocky road towards home. The self-same road where Jenna had had her accident. A collision with fate, that had snatched her from his prospective arms and into those of a blind man.

Around the next bend, he could see the cleft in the far ridge, where Shauna had died. Strangely, the memory seemed less real, less potent, less binding. An old restlessness reared suddenly in him. Perhaps it was time to part with the past and go looking for the future. But not here, in this place of old memories and lost hopes.

Just ahead, he saw the gates to the old manor house. The entrance light was on, and, in the driveway, he saw the low, sleek shape of the sporty car Fergusson used to drive to the city.

Anger rose like gall in his throat. He would leave Glenrae, he knew, but not before he settled a few old scores.

Turning in at the wide gates, he drove towards the house, bringing his Land Rover to rest alongside the gleaming plum-red car.

The front door was open to the biting night air and, tugging his collar up around his ears, Stuart squared his shoulders, crossed with long purposeful strides, and entered the house.

CHAPTER THIRTEEN

THERE were two envelopes on the hall mat as Jenna came downstairs. She let out a long sigh and hesitated before crossing to pick them up.

One of them she had been expecting, with the name of the school printed in the left hand corner. The other, also typewritten, seemed impersonal, until she saw the postmark of Glenrae. She smiled. Obviously, Louise had learned to use the small electric typewriter in the office. She put it to one side to be read later.

She took the first letter through into the kitchen, filling the electric kettle and switching on before sitting down at the kitchen table to open the envelope. Either way, she might be in need of a cup of tea when she'd read its contents. She was reluctant to draw the sheet of paper out and her hand trembled as she did so.

It was over two weeks since she'd had her interview, and as each day passed she had gradually lost hope. Even now, she couldn't open the crisp white sheet that would put an end to her ordeal of waiting, one way or another.

Since Stuart's visit, she'd been anxiously scanning the Situations Vacant, appalled to find them devoid of any single opening for a teacher. Consequently, this first and only interview had assumed a major importance. She found herself praying.

It had suddenly become imperative that she had a commitment, something to keep her here...something to stop her thinking about the alternative Stuart had suggested...a return to Glenrae. She must never allow herself to be tempted to go back.

The paper crackled as she opened it out. She knew, even before she'd read the short negative paragraph it contained, that she had failed, and, even though she'd steeled herself against failure, it was none the less painful.

Pushing the paper away, she lowered her head on to her arms and lay still, her eyes hot with unshed tears, longing suddenly for arms to comfort her...for a shoulder to cry on...for a chance to be weak, dependent, cared for.

After a long while, she thought of Louise's letter and rose wearily to get it. She needed her aunt's cheery chatter, although she knew that, in its own way, it brought added heartache.

She was surprised from her misery by the letterhead which emerged, announcing that it came from the Glenrae school board of directors. With a puzzled frown, she read the contents, inviting her to attend for interview. Its last paragraph advised her not to attempt the journey by car, but to take the train to the nearest station. Her expenses would be reimbursed and she would be met by arranged transport and driven to her destination. The letter was signed by Mrs Elizabeth McCullogh, secretary to the board.

Still disbelieving, she read it through a second time, noting a request for her to confirm the convenience of the arrangement.

Of course, it was all Stuart's doing. Jenna felt a reluctant warmth for his persistence. With a deep sigh, she sank back into her seat. Fate seemed to be conspiring against her.

After her recent disappointment, the offer was very tempting. The impersonal tone of the letter was reassuring, implying impartiality. Would there be any harm in going . . . just to find out what it entailed?

If Stuart was right, and there was a cottage to go with the job, then she could be quite independent of Louise's hospitality. She would be able to look after Suzie conveniently and wouldn't have to see too much of Stuart.

Duncan was no longer at the manor. Maybe he'd set up home with Marianne far away from Glenrae. In time, perhaps Glenrae would cease to be just a place of memories . . . of Duncan and her bitter-sweet summer . . . and become home.

Thinking of Suzie's sad face over the last few months, she felt a pang of guilt. Did she have the right to discard a chance of making the little girl happy again?

Jenna had been very careful to explain to Suzie that she was going to Glenrae on the chance of a job, not a cast-iron certainty of one, but her heart ached to see the joy shining out of her sister's face as she packed a small case for an overnight stay for both of them.

At the station, and all through the long journey, Suzie's excitement simmered beneath the surface, taking Jenna's mind off her own nervousness, as she tried to keep her sister's volatile spirits on an even keel.

Question after question kept bubbling from Suzie's lips.

'Will we be staying with Aunt Louise?'

'Shall I have time to ride?'

'Do you think Duncan would mind if I visited Midnight?'

Jenna steeled herself against the pain of that one and answered with as much patience as she could muster, breathing a deep sigh of relief as the train arrived at their destination at last.

A small number of passengers got off and Jenna stood uncertainly on the platform, wondering what form the transport arrangements promised in the letter would take.

The only vehicle in sight was a Land Rover parked in the compound just beyond the gate. Jenna's stomach did a double somersault at the sight of it, but in the next instant she was scolding herself. Surely she wasn't going to experience this reaction every time she saw such a vehicle. In the rough, mountainous terrain of the Highlands, Land Rovers were bound to be common.

But there was no mistaking the tall figure that came striding towards them, a familiar grim expression holding the darkly handsome face in granite hard lines.

Jenna's heart missed a beat and then lurched into a dizzying momentum. Her instinct was to turn and run as far away as possible, but Suzie was running towards Duncan, her squeals of delight ringing loudly in the empty station.

'Duncan! I knew you'd come to fetch us.'

With her teeth clamped tightly on her lower lip, Jenna stared helplessly at the approaching figure, mesmerised by the dark, glowering look he gave her above Suzie's bobbing curls. He bent to hug the ecstatic child, before gently putting her away from him.

Jenna swallowed hard and waited. Panic weighted her feet, gripped her whole body in a terrifying inertia. Only her eyes moved, lifting to his as he finally stood before her. For long seconds, she searched his gaze for some hint of his feelings, some clue as to how she might cope with this confrontation.

'Hello, Jenna,' he said quietly, making no move to touch her. 'Glad you could make it.'

Suddenly, she found her voice. 'What are you doing here? I was expecting someone from the school board.'

He raised a dark brow, his mouth curling cynically at one corner. 'I'm the chairman of the board of governors,' he said drily. 'You should feel honoured.'

Still the same cool, mocking tone...the same hard, unreadable eyes, she thought furiously. And this offer of a job was just another of his cruel hoaxes, designed to add to her hurt and humiliation.

'And you should feel ashamed,' she responded, fury flashing in icy fire from her violet-blue eyes. 'But I suppose that's too much to ask.'

Suddenly, he smiled. And it was as though the sun had come out unexpectedly on a cloudy day. His eyes gleamed.

'Still the same sweet, wild Jenna.'

He touched her hair, his long fingers gently capturing a tendril.

Jenna wanted to move back, to lash out at him, but found herself burning with hope at the unexpected tenderness in his eyes.

To her surprise, she felt herself drawn into his arms, her body bursting into flame as his mouth sweetly covered her own.

Her heart cried out that this was a trick—one she'd fallen for many times before—but its voice was drowned by the sound of its own beating.

He drew back to murmur against her burning lips. 'Welcome home.'

The next few moments had a dreamlike quality as he drew away from her and picked up the case. She watched him tweak Suzie's nose as she stared up at them both, a bemused expression on her small face.

'Come on,' he said. 'Let's go home.'

By the time they were all seated in the Land Rover, its large wheels eating up the miles, she had come slowly back to earth. What had he meant . . . 'let's go home'? Other questions crowded into her mind, and, though she was in no mood to wait for answers, she could see she would have to bide her time.

Duncan stared ahead, all his concentration centred on negotiating the narrow rocky roads she remembered so well. She was ashamed by the resurgent thrill she felt at the sight of his familiar profile and stifled an inward groan as she realised his power over her senses was as strong as ever.

Tearing her eyes from his face, she sat quietly, steeling herself for the ordeal she knew lay ahead. As the car took the remembered left turn, she realised that he was taking her to the manor and sat up, her breast heaving with apprehension.

'I'm supposed to be going to Glenrae for an interview,' she stormed, her fury increasing as she saw the sardonic curl of his mouth. 'It may come as a surprise to you, but I really need that job. If you do anything to jeopardise my chances of getting it, I'll never forgive you.'

'Relax.' He turned to her, a cool smile in his eyes. 'If you want the job, it's yours.'

The casual reply left her speechless. She'd suspected Stuart of being behind the offer, but how had Duncan become involved? She couldn't answer that question, nor another one which arose in its wake. What did Duncan hope to gain by kidnapping her again?

She wouldn't ask now and risk upsetting Suzie, but she would have her answers, she vowed, at the first available opportunity.

A welcoming committee awaited them at the manor. Suzie was bouncing up and down on the back seat as the Land Rover came to a halt at the front entrance and she was out of the vehicle and flinging herself into Annie's arms before Duncan had switched off the engine.

Mary was there too, and Jenna found it hard to swallow the huge lump which rose into her throat.

Duncan's hand gripped her elbow and he waved the women away irritably. 'Take young Suzie indoors. I want to talk to Jenna and I don't want to be disturbed.'

They disappeared obligingly and Jenna was left alone in the hallway with the man she had thought of almost incessantly since their first fateful meeting.

He all but dragged her into the sitting-room, where a bright log fire burned in the wide fireplace. As Jenna's eyes went to the french windows, seeking an avenue of escape if it should become necessary, she saw that soft, dancing snowflakes had begun to fall.

Duncan drew her down on to the settee, holding her firmly, while his eyes devoured her face.

'Why have you brought me here?' Jenna demanded breathlessly.

His gaze narrowed. 'Because this is where you belong.'

Jenna shivered, uncertain of him and unnerved by the way her mind kept being distracted to the curve of his mouth.

'I can't fight you any more, Duncan,' she said huskily.

'That's good news.' He smiled at her. 'Fighting isn't what I have in mind.'

His eyes smouldered dangerously, accelerating her pulse in an alarming way, but she managed to keep her voice low and steady.

'Perhaps you'd like to tell me what you *do* have in mind,' she invited. 'But I warn you . . . I don't intend to play any more games.'

'I'm glad to hear it.' He said. 'I'm surprised to hear *you've* been playing. I've always been deadly serious.'

'Always? Even when you asked me to marry you?' Jenna eyed him contemptuously. 'Do you think I don't know how you hated me? How much you wanted to hurt me?' She threw back her head proudly. 'But you can't do that any more.'

She heard him groan and saw his eyes darken as though in pain.

'I didn't hate *you*,' he said softly, and dropped his head into his hands. 'I suppose, at first, I hated the idea of your being with Anderson. I wanted to prevent him having what I thought I would never have again . . . happiness.'

He looked up suddenly, his eyes seeking hers. 'It's true, I wanted revenge. But then I wanted you. Above all and everything else, I wanted you.'

'You *wanted* me,' she echoed bitterly. 'Even that day in the cottage . . . when we made love . . . that's all it was . . . sexual desire.'

'You're wrong.'

He drew her into the circle of his arms. She went unresisting, but lay against him tense and unyielding, until he began a gentle stroking of her hair.

'Damn it, I have to admit,' he swore softly, 'that's all I *intended* it to be.' He smiled crookedly, turning her heart over. 'Believe me, I fought tooth and nail to keep it that way.' His eyes, searching hers, glowed with tenderness. 'But I was fighting against myself all the way. I couldn't win.'

Her whole body was beginning to melt and she turned her face into the hollow of his broad shoulder.

'Oh, Duncan,' she sighed. 'If only I could believe this wasn't just another of your tricks.'

He drew her closer. 'If I could convince you, would you forgive me . . . trust me?'

He bent his head, his lips descending on hers, sweet and devouring, making her throat ache and tears spill on to her cheeks.

'Why did you stay away so long?' she whispered. There was no point now in pride. 'I was hoping you'd come to find me.'

He pulled back to look at her. 'God knows I wanted to. It took every ounce of strength I possessed to keep me away from you.'

'But why . . . ?'

'I thought you were in love with Anderson. You said you were going to marry him. You even risked your neck climbing down that tree to get back to him.'

Jenna groaned. Her own lies had caused her misery—kept him away from her.

'Then, when Anderson told me you were in love with me, I began to believe again what I'd seen in your eyes, felt in your body when we made love.'

She pulled away, a startled expression on her face. 'You've spoken to Stuart? About me?'

'He did mention you in passing. After we'd exchanged initial pleasantries and some home truths.'

To her astonishment, Duncan's face showed rueful amusement.

He rubbed reminiscently at his chin.

'You fought?' Jenna stared at him in amazement. 'With Stuart?'

He nodded. 'A token blood-letting for both parties. After which he put me right about a number of things.'

The shock took her breath away. Even now, she couldn't believe this whole thing wasn't some new, subtle kind of torture he'd invented.

'You've forgiven Stuart?'

He grimaced. 'He convinced me there was nothing to forgive.'

He rubbed a hand across his eyes in a weary gesture, lost to her for a few moments as he explored the past. 'It's taken me a while to forgive myself.'

She knew he was thinking of Shauna and her tragedy, and hoped he would find it hurt less as time went by.

After a while, he seemed to shake himself back to the present.

'Did you plan with Stuart to lure me back to Glenrae?' Jenna asked, wishing she'd been spared this extra pain.

'Not exactly. Anderson called in to see me on his way back from visiting you. He admitted he'd gone hoping to persuade you to marry him, but gave up, because he thought you were in love with me.'

Jenna bit her lip. So she'd been that transparent!

Duncan smiled darkly. 'I won't repeat what threats he made if I hurt you again, because it will never happen.'

'But...the job...' Jenna prompted in confusion.

He nodded. 'Anderson told me he'd mentioned it to you and asked me to put your name forward. As chairman of the board I would naturally have to know anyway. It seemed a good way of getting you up here so that I could talk to you, but it wasn't a trick. The job does exist and it's yours if you want it.'

'I do want it.' Jenna confirmed. 'But aren't there other candidates?'

'One or two. But I'm sure you'll outshine them. After all, you've taught me one or two things...'

His arms came around her again and he cupped her cheek gently.

'But, wouldn't you rather marry me instead?'

Jenna bit her lip. 'I don't know...if I could be sure there...weren't any ghosts...'

He stared at her, not understanding. Then, as her meaning became clear, his expression changed.

'There won't be any ghosts, Jenna. The past is buried.' His eyes darkened. 'And I might as well do the same with my future, if you won't share it with me.'

He reached for her, but she resisted him.

'What about Marianne? She told Stuart you were going to marry her. That's partly why I wasn't sure about your proposal.'

He shook his head in vexation. 'She knew better than that. I was always honest.'

Jenna was surprised by a feeling of compassion for the girl she had thought was her rival. 'Poor Marianne. Where is she now?'

Duncan shrugged. 'I don't know. She went off in a huff when she realised your going away made no difference to the way I felt about her.' Sudden amusement gleamed in his eyes. 'But it wouldn't surprise me if that cousin of yours knows. I always did think they might be kindred souls.' His hand gripped her waist. 'She accused me of being in love with you.'

Jenna stilled. It was the first time he had mentioned love.

'She was wrong, of course,' Jenna said drily, but with a flutter of uncertainty.

He laughed. 'No. She was right. She saw it almost from the start...what I was too pig-headed to admit to myself. I loved you practically from the first moment I saw you. But I couldn't let it happen . . . not with the cousin of a man like Anderson.' He shook his head. 'The only way I could touch you . . . kiss you . . . was to pretend to myself that I was punishing you. But I was only punishing myself. Each kiss . . . each embrace . . . only increased my desire for you . . . and yet I seemed to be pushing you further and further away . . . out of my reach. I couldn't stand the thought of losing you. More and more, it became impossible for me to let you go.'

Jenna gave a rueful smile. 'So you locked me in the bedroom to make sure.'

He coloured faintly. 'A bit desperate, I admit. But at the time, it seemed the only way to get you to take me seriously. I never meant to keep you prisoner— only to give you time to think.'

'Perhaps that's what I need now.'

Jenna's head swam with confusion. She pulled herself from him and stood up, restlessly pacing to the window to stare out.

The gentle snow shower had turned into a blizzard and already the white carpet was inches deep.

Duncan came and stood behind her, his hand resting on her shoulder. She could feel his warmth and the movement of his breath in her hair.

'It looks as though you might have to make up your mind in a hurry,' he murmured. 'If this blizzard keeps up, we could be snowed in for months.' He turned her to face him, his eyes glowing with bright flame. 'When the snow melts, we might just *have* to get married.'

Jenna laughed shakily. 'Are you sure you didn't organise the weather too? As another way of forcing me into marriage.'

His smile vanished and his gaze became intense. 'There will be no more force, Jenna. Possibly for the first time in my life, I want someone else's happiness before my own. I love you and I want you.'

Jenna shook her head, unwilling to deliver herself finally into his hands. 'I still can't believe you mean this. I'm so used to thinking that you hate me.'

He took her hand and carried it to his warm lips. Her whole body tingled with the vibrations he set up.

'Let me prove to you that I love you, Jenna.' His eyes looked deep into hers, their bright light pushing away the shadows. 'It's taken me a long time to prove it to myself.'

Jenna's heart swelled with sudden hope. Was it possible it was really true after all?

He took her into his arms to kiss her lips gently, and then, as she offered no resistance, with growing demand, moving persuasively against the soft contours of her mouth until she began to tremble. He growled softly and drew her more closely into his embrace.

With a sigh, she relaxed against him, letting the tide of her feelings sweep away her doubts. She was where she had wanted to be almost from the first day... in his arms.

'Say you love me, Jenna,' he demanded softly.

'I love you,' she whispered, and then gasped as he kissed her again... a kiss filled with passionate exultation.

She'd come home... a stranger no more to his house... and his heart.

The journey had been a rocky one, but she'd finally found her road into paradise.

Next Month's Romances

Each month you can choose from a wide variety of romance with Mills & Boon. Below are the new titles to look out for next month, why not ask either Mills & Boon Reader Service or your Newsagent to reserve you a copy of the titles you want to buy — just tick the titles you would like and either post to Reader Service or take it to any Newsagent and ask them to order your books.

Please save me the following titles:	Please tick	√
RIDE THE STORM	Emma Darcy	
A DAUGHTER'S DILEMMA	Miranda Lee	
PRIVATE LIVES	Carole Mortimer	
THE WAYWARD WIFE	Sally Wentworth	
HAUNTING ALLIANCE	Catherine George	
RECKLESS CRUSADE	Patricia Wilson	
CRY WOLF	Amanda Carpenter	
LOVE IN TORMENT	Natalie Fox	
STRANGER PASSING BY	Lilian Peake	
PRINCE OF DARKNESS	Kate Proctor	
A BRIDE FOR THE TAKING	Sandra Marton	
JOY BRINGER	Lee Wilkinson	
A WOMAN'S LOVE	Grace Green	
DANGEROUS DOWRY	Catherine O'Connor	
WEB OF FATE	Helena Dawson	
A FAMILY AFFAIR	Charlotte Lamb	

If you would like to order these books in addition to your regular subscription from Mills & Boon Reader Service please send £1.70 per title to: Mills & Boon Reader Service, P.O. Box 236, Croydon, Surrey, CR9 3RU, quote your Subscriber No:..
(If applicable) and complete the name and address details below. Alternatively, these books are available from many local Newsagents including W.H.Smith, J.Menzies, Martins and other paperback stockists from 6th November 1992.

Name:...

Address:...

....Post Code:...........................

To Retailer: If you would like to stock M&B books please contact your regular book/magazine wholesaler for details.

You may be mailed with offers from other reputable companies as a result of this application. If you would rather not take advantage of these opportunities please tick box ☐

WIN A TRIP TO ITALY

Three lucky readers and their partners will spend a romantic weekend in Italy next May. You'll stay in a popular hotel in the centre of Rome, perfectly situated to visit the famous sites by day and enjoy the food and wine of Italy by night. During the weekend we are holding our first International Reader Party, an exciting celebratory event where you can mingle with Mills & Boon fans from all over Europe and meet some of our top authors.

HOW TO ENTER

We'd like to know just how wonderfully romantic your partner is, and how much Mills & Boon means to you.

Firstly, answer the questions below and then fill in our tie-breaker sentence:

1. **Which is Rome's famous ancient ruin?**

   ☐ The Parthenon   ☐ The Colosseum   ☐ The Sphinx

2. **Who is the famous Italian opera singer?**

   ☐ Nana Mouskouri   ☐ Julio Iglesias   ☐ Luciano Pavarotti

3. **Which wine comes from Italy?**

   ☐ Frascati   ☐ Liebfraumilch   ☐ Bordeaux

Tie-Breaker: Well just how romantic is your man? Does he buy you chocolates, send you flowers, take you to romantic candlelit restaurants? Send us a recent snapshot of the two of you (passport size is fine), together with a caption which tells us in no more than 15 words what makes your romantic man so special you'd like to visit Rome with him as the weekend guests of Mills & Boon.

....

....

....

....

Mills & Boon

In order to find out more about how much Mills & Boon means to you, we'd like you to answer the following questions:

1. How long have you been reading Mills & Boon books?

☐ One year or less ☐ 2-5 years ☐ 6-10 years

☐ 10 years or more

2. Which series do you usually read?

☐ Mills & Boon Romances ☐ Medical Romances ☐ Best Seller

☐ Temptation ☐ Duet ☐ Masquerade

3. How often do you read them? ☐ 1 a month or less

☐ 2-4 a month ☐ 5-10 a month ☐ More than 10 a month

Please complete the details below and send your entry to: Mills & Boon Reader Service, FREEPOST, P.O. Box 236, Croydon, Surrey CR9 9EL, England.

Name: ....

Address: ....

.... Post Code: ....

Are you a Reader Service subscriber?

☐ No ☐ Yes my Subscriber No. is: ....
